For my wife Angela and our children Aaron, Adele and Lucy,
our grandchildren Georgia, Ethan, Jacob, Joely, Summer,
our new great-granddaughter Ivey May and my brother Ken.

BOWIE, CAMBO
&
ALL THE HYPE

JOHN CAMBRIDGE

M^cNIDDER | &
GRACE

Cambo
22

Published by McNidder & Grace
21 Bridge Street
Carmarthen SA31 3JS
Wales, United Kingdom

www.mcnidderandgrace.com

Original paperback first published 2021
© John Cambridge

Every effort has been made to obtain necessary permission with reference to
copyright material. The publisher apologises if, inadvertently, any sources
remain unacknowledged and will be glad to make the necessary arrangements
at the earliest opportunity.

Image credits: cover photo, pp.133–34; colour section p.11 bottom, pp.13,
14, 15 top, p.16 top, Angela Cambridge. Page 54 and colour section p.3,
Kevin Cann. Colour section pp.8–9, Ray Stevenson. Page 40 and colour
section p.11 top, Ian Gibson. Page 122, Tony Visconti. Colour section p.16
bottom, Tracey Taylor.

A catalogue record for this work is available from the British Library.

ISBN 9780857162168 paperback
ISBN 9780857162175 ebook

Editor: Garry Burnett
Cover: Tabitha Palmer
Designer: JS Typesetting Ltd
Printed and bound in the United Kingdom by Short Run Press, Exeter

Praise for *Bowie, Cambo & All the Hype*

'A warm, engaging first-hand account of a pivotal time in David Bowie's career, full of fascinating insight and turn-of-the-'70s detail.'
Rob Hughes, music journalist, *Uncut*

'You were a great player in that early transition from David's acoustic sound to the full-on rock sound that eventually gave birth to Ziggy. You have a big story to tell.'
Tony Visconti, record producer, musician and singer

'I know how much you have meant to David.
Iman Bowie

'There is no doubt about it; with that extended gesture of friendship and belief (in both David Bowie and Mick Ronson) John Cambridge single-handedly altered the trajectory of popular music.'
Kevin Cann, Bowie authority, author and designer

'History is full of 'What if's'. What if Lennon had never met McCartney. What If Elvis never became entangled with the conniving Colonel Tom Parker. And what if John Cambridge had never uttered the words 'Mick' and 'Ronson' within hearing distance of David Bowie. His book is full of enthusiasm, pathos, John's infectious good nature and humour… and almost inevitably a fair few What if's. It needed to be written. Thanks John.'
Marc Riley, BBC Radio 6

'David Bowie created a brilliant public persona in which you were never sure what was true and what was artifice. His work will be discussed for generations and he will remain a major influence on new performers. It is excellent that somebody as close to him as Cambo should present his own take on that rise to fame.'
Spencer Leigh, author and journalist

'Behind every great man are a great many friends. John 'Cambo' Cambridge was one of Bowie's greatest friends.'
Will Sergeant, Echo & the Bunnymen

'Cambo plays killer wig-out drums on one of my all-time favourite recordings, the radio session of March '70 when he, Bowie, Ronson and Visconti laid down the blueprint not just for that mighty song of songs 'The Width Of A Circle' but for the rest of 1970s rock'n'roll through prog, glam, punk and beyond.'
Mike Scott, The Waterboys

'A remarkable and heartfelt memoir from someone who was there.'
David Quantick, music writer

FOREWORD

The entertainment industry, just like any other walk of life, is littered with 'What if?' stories; some are even legends. One of my favourite music industry 'what if?' comes directly from the man who wrote this book, Mr John Cambridge no less. It is, of course, *the* story of John introducing Ronson to Bowie and his personal battle to encourage a reluctant Hull gardener (and respected semi-pro musician) down to London to meet a sceptical up-and-coming pop singer.

The soap opera that then ensued after John first recommended his old friend Mick Ronson to David Bowie and his producer Tony Visconti you will get to in this book and it's quite something, littered with – not just one – but many 'What if?' moments; moments that, in the main, pivoted around John himself. And at any point of his fascinating recollection you can be forgiven for thinking, 'Just give up on it John! They don't deserve you.' But he didn't.

Bear in mind, when John left London for Hull that day David had still not actually said to John, "Okay then, bring him down." John had simply given up asking and decided to take matters into his own hands.

Now this isn't to say that, without this particular intervention and its impact on David's creativity we wouldn't still be talking about David Bowie today, because I'm sure we would. A talent like that was already primed, fuelled and ready to launch. But, if you were to totally exclude Mick Ronson from that final equation, and at such a crucial time in David's development, it would certainly have made David's story much poorer. That's unequivocal.

And what would have become of *The Man Who Sold The World*, *Hunky Dory*, *Ziggy Stardust*, *Aladdin Sane* and *Pin Ups* without Mick? These albums, of course, have his gifted dabs all over them like an indelible watermark.

It just makes you wonder though, what if John Cambridge had given up at any point during that testing week in early 1970?

What if?

There is no doubt about it, however; with that extended gesture of friendship and belief (in both David and Mick) John Cambridge single-handedly altered the trajectory of popular music.

The same question then, could also be applied to John's dismissal from David's band at another pivotal moment. What might have happened if John had remained the drummer in Bowie's band? For that you will find John's own candid answer in this book. In fact, it is a very frank answer in a no-nonsense memoir, a story that I thought I was pretty familiar with myself. But there are always things to learn for us all. And, while working on this book, even John discovered a few things he was previously unaware of before he started putting pen to paper (which is often the nature of things when our stories become so interwoven with the lives of others).

Over the years we have known each other, John has always, without fail, been there when I needed him. Whether it was to answer a string of questions for my own projects, or for the various live events I invited him to be part of, John has always been fully supportive. It's therefore been a pleasure to finally return a little bit of that support for an important project of his own.

It's certainly been an entertaining read too.

Kevin Cann
July 2021

CONTENTS

INTRODUCTION

Here we go again! Another book on David Bowie, I hear you say. Somebody else trying to cash in? Well, I promise you, this will not be like any other Bowie book you read.

At home I have a large cardboard box full of other people's books and magazines, mostly about David. Some have been gratefully signed by their authors as a thank you for me helping them with their research and lending a bit of weight to their writing, checking, adding or correcting details when I thought they weren't quite accurate or were incomplete. Over the years, I've always given my time freely and willingly to talk about this remarkable time in my life.

My kids have been urging me for many years to write down all of my stories too, and to bring out my own book, but up until now, I could never really be arsed. I suppose, being able to say you were friends with David Bowie for nearly 50 years would be a good enough reason for most people to put pen to paper (although admittedly there were some large breaks in us keeping in touch), and being partly responsible for, or a witness to, some of the most important breakthrough moments in his career does make you seem, in some people's eyes, really important.

I was there when David went through some significant rites of passage. When he had his first big hit with 'Space Oddity', when he got married, when he played his first Glam Rock gig, when he passed his driving test, when his father died, when he celebrated his 50th birthday, etc. I am also one of the few people who can say I shared a car, a dressing room, and even a bed with him!

I was good friends with someone who was later to become one of the most famous, iconic faces of the twentieth century. Someone who would alter the course of rock and pop music, fashion, media and people's attitudes towards diversity, tolerance and sexuality. Someone who, when I knew him, was always just a mate.

And that's what he was, to most of us who knew him then. Granted, he was a very talented mate, who also liked a laugh and a joke, the occasional water pistol fight or kick-around with a football in the garden at Haddon Hall, but who was still finding his way professionally when I drummed for him at the end of the '60s and the beginning of the '70s.

I'm proud to say he was someone who remained a mate right until the end, despite all the craziness that happened in between. David and I never had a cross word and at every reunion or contact we always seemed to pick up where we'd left off. I feel that the time to write about it is definitely right now – before the ageing process gets in the way!

Readers might be surprised at some of the other memories I've included here and some of the bands that shared the bill, such as Pink Floyd, Rod Stewart, Free, Genesis Black Sabbath and Fleetwood Mac, and some of the famous musicians I met or shared a dressing room with, such as Jeff Beck, Robert Palmer, Ozzy Osborne, Jon Anderson and Jimi Hendrix.

Ken Pitt, David's ex-manager, was probably the first person to ask me for help with a book, *The Pitt Report*, in 1982 and rang me out of the blue to ask if I could remember a few dates I did with David. 'Do you remember when you did such and such?' he asked. 'Was it between January and February 1970?'. And I could confidently reply: 'I can tell you exactly when it was because I kept a diary of every gig I have ever done, not just with David.' And it's true, beginning with the Regal Rooms, ABC Cinema, Hull on Thursday, 10 December 1964 (teatime, a children's party with my first band The Gonx), and right through to the present day.

This attention to detail is another reason I have been consulted so often by Bowie biographers, who frequently get the timing, personnel, events, conversations and even years wrong. I'll refer to some of those as we go through the book – and hope this will be my opportunity to set the record straight on certain important details.

People sometimes ask me how David's name is pronounced. It is exactly the same as the 'bow eey' knife (as in '*bow* and arrows' or 'rain*bow*') and that was the pronunciation he used and preferred. He told me once that he got the name from the 1960 John Wayne film *The Alamo*, which featured Richard Widmark as Jim Bowie, the man who made famous the Bowie fighting knife.

Sometimes in this book I'll refer to him by his Christian name 'David' and sometimes as 'Bowie' because, well, that's what we did at the time. It's not about me being inconsistent or over-familiar. Sometimes we just called him 'Dave' (Angie Bowie refers to him as 'Davey'). In the same way, I'll sometimes refer to Mick Ronson as 'Mick' and sometimes as 'Ronno' because that's what we called him. It was his nickname and he even called a band after it.

And finally, a very good friend gave me some advice about how I should actually go about writing this. 'Do it for your family, your kids, and grandkids,' he said. And he was right, it's much easier when you have somebody in mind – so I am imagining that they are all in front of me, now. After all, they are the ones who have been urging me to write it all down. So, here we go.

This is for them.

Chapter 1
MY HOME AND MY FAMILY

My family come from the North of England. Marjorie Mary Getliffe, my mother, was from Manchester and Tom Cambridge, my dad, from Goldthorpe, a small mining town between Doncaster and Barnsley – just ten miles from where David Bowie's father, Haywood Stenton 'John' Jones was born, five years earlier than dad in 1912.

I often wonder, and others have speculated too, if maybe David felt the Yorkshire 'Northern' connection between us and that's one of the reasons we got on so well. It does seem a bit of a coincidence that so many other people involved with his early career came from Yorkshire too, including his Feathers bandmate John 'Hutch' Hutchinson; Trevor, Mick and Woody, the three Spiders from Mars; and Bowie's former bodyguard Stuey George, who was also our roadie in the band The Rats and whom I still see occasionally.

Even Gary Miller who produced the track 'Everyone Says "Hi"', a much later Bowie hit from the *Heathen* album, was a Hull lad too. Later in the book I will describe the time David and Angie Bowie came 'up north' to stay with us in our little flat in Hull and my parents' reaction to that.

Mam and Dad met while they were in the army and were married in Salford just after the Second World War. My brother Ken was born on 25 May 1946. I was born down Albany Street on Spring Bank in Hull on 8 May 1949.

Dad originally moved to Hull with his elder brother Bill after the Second World War as the city had been badly bombed in the

Dad and Mam Cambridge with son Aaron

John with brother Ken

Blitz. He was a plasterer by trade and there was plenty of work to be had rebuilding the city.

I remember Dad telling me all these amazing stories about the war, and how, as a prisoner of war in Italy, he had escaped, only to be captured and then to escape again. I was always saying to him, 'You ought to write a book about your life.' It seemed to be just one adventure after another and something which was actually worth writing down.

His answer was much the same as mine used to be ('I can't be arsed!') even though his achievements were far more notable than mine. Mine are mostly about music, football, running pubs or working on building sites, not to mention the all-important family life.

I often wonder about what my Dad had to do when he was 22, the year the Second World War broke out, compared to what a typical 22-year-old has to do nowadays and compared to what I'd done by that age – virtually nothing.

Dad was a massive influence on my life and if he was still around, he would no doubt give his own, typically down-to-earth take on the Bowies' stay with us in Hull: how they ran up a big telephone bill, smoked his fags and how he may have provided David with inspiration for some of his most famous lyrics.

One thing I will always remember about Dad is that he was an avid reader; mostly paperback novels, potboilers, cowboy stories, war sagas, etc. which he used to buy from the West Hull Bookshop near Madeley Street off Hessle Road. My mam would go and collect five or six at a time, at a shilling a book, and when he'd finished she'd take them back and swap them for five or six more.

She kept doing this for years to the point where nobody knew what he'd read and what he hadn't. Sometimes I'd go shopping with her on Hessle Road, pick up a book and ask: 'Has he had that one, Mam?', only to find when we got back that he'd usually already read five out of the six we'd got for him.

If he knew I was writing a book, he would probably say something like: 'Son, you don't have to put big words in a book to make it interesting; big words like "wheelbarrow", "lighthouse" and "marmalade". And don't forget, never use a big word when a diminutive one will suffice'. (As you can see, I inherited my dad's sense of humour.)

Dad died in 1981 – if he somehow finds out I need a ghost writer, I'm sure he'll be the first to be in touch.

Sense of humour was another one of the reasons David Bowie and I got on so well, and our South Yorkshire fathers would probably have enjoyed a pint together and had a lot in common too.

We lived in a couple of other bedsits after Albany Street, before eventually moving into a council flat into Brisbane Street, in 1954. We were within easy walking distance of both the city centre and the shops and pubs of the famous Hessle Road trawling and fishing community, which was Hull's main industry at the time.

Our flat was brand new in a three-storey block; we were its first tenants.

Although it was modern, it didn't have many modern facilities. There was no central heating, just one coal fire in the lounge with a back boiler attached, which meant if you wanted hot water you had to pull the damper out under the fire to heat the water. In winter the bedrooms could get pretty cold and even though my mam and dad had a little two-bar electric fire, they would normally only ever have one bar on to save money.

And these were the days when you had to put a shilling in the meter too. It was less than ten years after the Second World War and the devastation, especially in Hull and within striking distance of the docks, was still to be seen on the streets all around in the rubble and the bombed buildings.

Dad's army gear was still about the flat too, especially his tin hat and great army overcoat. My brother Ken and I used to share a bed then, as brothers often did; a big metal frame with springs that could be bounced up and down on like a trampoline. In cold winter weather, we'd sometimes get frost on the inside of the window and Mam used to put Dad's army greatcoat on the bed as a top cover for extra warmth.

One night when we'd gone to bed, I shouted through to her, 'Mam, our Ken's pulling the big coat over to his side and he won't give me any of it!' She came rushing in.

'Will you be quiet!' she said. 'Your Auntie Maud's here.' (We had loads of aunties in Hull, most of whom weren't our real aunties.) 'She's only in the front room and she can hear you both, so stop showing me up! Anyway, it's not a coat, it's an eiderdown.' And off she went, back through to the front room.

Ten minutes later I shouted through again, 'Mam, Ken's just ripped the sleeve off the eiderdown.'

Many people in Hull used to have photos taken at Jerome's on Whitefriargate – in the '50s and '60s as you can see. They are the ones who provided the cowboy suit in the photo – a shape of things to come!

John – Cowboyman Jnr

My nickname was always Cambo (pronounced 'came bow', as in 'bow tie') and it has stuck with me for most of my life. When Angie Bowie wrote to Mum and Dad, she even called them 'Mum and Dad Cambo'!

When David and Angie Bowie came to stay in our Brisbane Street flat, in February 1970, they slept in that same room Ken and I had shared, in that same cold bed.

I first became properly interested in music while I was a pupil at Saint Wilfred's Catholic School on Saner Street, next to the Boulevard. When I was aged about ten, I used to bang on my little school desk with rulers, constantly drill the tabletop with my fingers or use my mam's knitting needles to batter the cardboard covers of *Beano* annuals placed on my bedspread to look like a drum kit. It was as if the drummer inside of me was impatient to get out.

I had a fairly normal, happy and uneventful childhood, really. I have always liked sport, especially football, and as a 'black and whiter' I was always a keen supporter of Hull FC rugby league club.

My big brother Ken was a big influence on me growing up. He was three years older, and it was through him I first got to listen to many of the big stars of the day. Stars like Eddie Cochran, Johnny Kidd & the Pirates and of course the King, Elvis.

My mam and dad were going to get me an electric train set for Christmas when I was 12, but Ken persuaded me to ask for a joint present of a Dansette record player, as they could never have afforded both. That Dansette was to play a big part in my musical education right through the '60s. I'd plug it in in the bedroom, close the door and play along on my *Beano* annuals in time to the likes of 'Glad All Over' by the Dave Clark Five, 'Linda Lu' by Johnny Kidd & the Pirates and 'F.B.I.' and 'Man of Mystery' by The Shadows.

By the time I was about 14, I used to go regularly to nearby Madeley Street Baths on roller-skating nights, where basically all you did was skate round on the boarded-over swimming baths on old roller skates that you hired for the night. (Only the posh kids had their own roller skates). Once again music was a big factor, especially in 1963, which was a momentous time for music in this country, and the world.

In this year the Beatles continued their domination of the charts with 'Please, Please Me', following up 'Love Me Do', their big hit of the previous year. Meanwhile, down in the capital, an unknown teenager called David Jones recorded his first demo single 'I Never Dreamed' with The Konrads.

My brother Ken took his copy of the Beatles' 'Please, Please Me' to the skating sessions to give the elderly DJ in a tuxedo his first taste of the Fab Four. Other groups had begun to break through on the pop scene too, especially the Rolling Stones, The Searchers and The Hollies, and I would go to my bedroom, knitting needles in hand (the thicker, the better), to practise tapping along to the beat of their latest releases.

At this stage I'd still never played on a real drum kit. In fact, I don't think I'd even seen one close up either. In desperation I even sent away for brochures and catalogues with pictures of drums in them so I could study them.

Everything changed when I started going to the so-called Beat clubs in Hull. It was a busy and active scene for live music in the early '60s in Hull and I remember particularly the Gondola Club in Little Queen Street and the Kontiki Club in Whitefriargate, both in the town centre. These clubs would be packed out, especially on weekends at the Gondola, when we would be treated to acts such as The Grease Band (featuring Joe Cocker) and other famous acts just breaking through. There was always a surcharge on the door at the Gondola for the 'name' bands, but it was also a place where decent local bands could cut their teeth playing live.

I became an enthusiastic regular and, as the Kontiki wasn't licensed, a kid my age could also get a burger and soft drink and relax to enjoy live music by the many local up-and-coming performers. And, of course, it also meant an opportunity for me to study some real drum kits and get familiar with the local drummers, their techniques and their repertoires.

One night at the Kontiki, a group from the East Yorkshire town of Driffield, called The Roadrunners, came back to play their second set after going to the pub in the break. Their drummer was late getting back, so the rest of the band stood on stage waiting for him, ready to go, and I could see the crowd were getting a bit twitchy.

One of my mates shouted: 'John'll stand in while he comes back, won't you, John?' And even though I didn't have any knitting needles with me, I said: 'Oh yes' – and was a bit surprised when the singer said: 'Come on then. Do you know "Mona"?'

I'd only ever heard the Rolling Stones' cover of the song, which fortunately happened to be the version that they did. It turned out to be quite an easy one to play, though, with a kind of thumping beat required on the floor tom-tom. It dawned on me halfway through the performance that I didn't have the equivalent of a bass drum on the *Beano* annual set-up, so I really surprised myself to find I kept hitting the bass drum pedal instinctively throughout the song.

It turned out that Mick 'Woody' Woodmansey, who replaced me in both The Rats and with David Bowie, also joined The Roadrunners after their drummer had left – another one of many remarkable coincidences in my career. At the end of my debut, I got a round of applause from the band (and my mates) – possibly because their drummer had returned, possibly because I hadn't made an arse of myself.

Either way, my career as a drummer had begun!

A few weeks later virtually the same scenario occurred again (bloody late drummers), this time with a group from Scarborough called The Incas, only now the song was a lot harder to play.

'"Long Tall Sally"?' the lead singer asked, as I, now an experienced live performer, nodded confidently, thinking that the Beatles' version I knew was the only version there was.

At this stage, I wrongly assumed that Lennon and McCartney had written all their own songs.

Even being generous I would probably give myself no more than two out of ten. Off we went, stopped, started, stopped again and then went at it like the bloody clappers. I suppose the best I could say is: 'I got through it', but at least it now made me want to master the instrument and finally get my own proper drum kit.

I'd actually seen one in a second-hand shop in Midland Street, not far from us, in Hull. It was a worn, battered, white assortment of drums and looked very old-fashioned, but as far as I was concerned it was definitely the one for me. After walking past it every weekend on my way to the city centre, I finally plucked up courage to go in and ask how much it was.

'Fifteen quid,' the shopkeeper said, which at the time was right out of my reach.

The next step was to get round my dad.

There were some amazing, inspirational drummers around at that time. There were no big arenas yet, so in smaller venues there were plenty of opportunities to get really close up to see all the best local players in action – such as Adrian Gatie of The Aces and Jim Simpson, who also played in The Rats when Mick Ronson was a member, as well as many visiting future legends.

In 1963 at Hull City Hall, I saw 'up close' no less than the Rolling Stones, who weren't even top of the bill that night but had just had a hit with Chuck Berry's 'Come On'.

Top of the bill was reserved for Johnny 'Shakin' All Over' Kidd & the Pirates and The Aces (another top local band), supported by Heinz & the Saints (formerly of The Tornados). Although the gig was sold out, I managed to get a special, cheap rear-view seat, actually on the stage and behind the bands. Most people would have been disappointed, but I was in my element because I was right next to the drummer – just a wheelbarrow's distance from Charlie Watts! I remember going to the toilets behind the stage and excusing myself to Mick Jagger and the band who were waiting in the wings as I squeezed by: 'Sorry, but I'm busting for a piss.'

I was beginning to collect autographs at this point, and that night managed to get Johnny Kidd & the Pirates (without even bothering to ask The Stones). Years later, when I finally got David Bowie to sign my book (it would have felt a bit daft asking him when I lived with him), he was really interested in some of the other names in it too, many of whom were his heroes.

I failed my eleven plus so was unable to go to the Catholic grammar school. Instead, I stayed at St Wilfred's RC School until 1964 and left when I was just fifteen. My dad got me a job as an apprentice plasterer with him, and as I was now starting to get a regular income, I thought it was finally time to invest in a drum kit of my own.

After years of tapping my scratched and scored *Beano* annuals, it was time to act.

I had made my mind up I wanted to play in a band and now, with the means to pay, Dad and I went to Gough & Davy, which at the time was the biggest music store in Hull, to look at some kits and sort out hire purchase (HP) terms on this impressive red 'sparkle' kit I'd seen in the window.

My dad signed the HP papers but after a few days we had a letter to say our application had been rejected because of what would nowadays be classed as a 'poor payment history'. My dad was livid, seeing as we'd never had any bad credit in the past, so naturally he wanted to know the details from the finance company. Imagine his shock when he was told he'd bought a pram, cot and highchair six months before and never paid for them.

'Who for?' he said, irate. 'John? He's only fifteen and we've no grandkids! Why would I want a load of baby gear?'

The finance company discovered that a friend or relation of the people in the flat below had nicked my dad's identity to buy all the baby gear items. We'd never actually seen the correspondence or paperwork that went with it, which I can only assume had been somehow intercepted by them.

Once this was sorted out, Gough & Davy's got back in touch to say that as far as they were concerned the deal was back on, but by this point my dad had ceased negotiations and told them to 'stick

J.P. Cornells, Hull (1964), the shop where John bought his first Trixon drum kit and later his Ludwig drums. Mick Ronson also bought his famous Gibson Les Paul custom here

their drums up their arse'. Instead we went to Cornell's on Spring Bank, the other big music shop in Hull, where Mick Ronson bought the Les Paul guitar he used with Bowie and many others.

So in 1964 I picked out a shiny new grey Trixon kit and cymbals, costing a lot more than the selection from Gough & Davy, and carried it upstairs to our first floor flat. Now, the flat on Brisbane Street was sandwiched between a flat above and a flat below (and on either side!), and within about five minutes of hitting my drums for the first time the neighbours must have realised that this wasn't just the Dansette turned up a bit louder, and a frantic thumping and banging on the walls and ceiling quickly followed.

I could have been forgiven for saying 'revenge is sweet' after the HP incident, but this now left me with two main problems: where do I practise and how do I get into a group?

For now, unfortunately, it was back to the *Beanos*.

I knew I wanted to be in a band as soon as I began to get into music. I can sing reasonable harmonies (I even sang backing vocals on David's 'Memory of a Free Festival') and I can also play a few basic guitar chords, but I always knew that being a drummer was going to be my musical vocation. As I've said, 1963 was quite a year in the history of rock and roll music, and, coincidentally, it was the year before my own musical career kick-started. I was just 15 when I joined my first group, a local band called The Gonx.

I'd now begun attending Monday nights at the Locarno Ballroom (the Mecca Ballroom) in Hull, and was completely besotted and influenced by Beat group sounds. Despite having a good natural sense of rhythm, I never felt the urge to get on the dance floor, though, and much preferred wandering around with my mates, eyeing up the girls.

My public debut as a drummer had now turned into an uncontrollable itch to get into my own band – and when I saw an advert in the *Hull Daily Mail* small ads entertainment section for a local 'rhythm and blues group seeking a drummer', it seemed that opportunity had finally arrived.

Some people might find it hard to believe that I am naturally shy (I am), but when I answered the ad I was so nervous I concocted this story about 'my mate John' who had 'just bought a set of drums and who was looking to join a group.'

'Oh yes,' I continued, now completely getting into the part. 'He's just bought his own kit and I think he would be really interested. Why don't you give him a ring?'

My thinking at the time was that I would save a bit of face if they did audition and reject me. I could always say, 'Well, it was you who rang me first!'

When they did call to arrange the audition, I even put on a different voice and agreed to be at the Railway Club in Hull (now the Tiger's Lair) on the following Saturday morning. The group's roadie was also the singer's dad, so he picked me up early to take me and my kit to the audition room on Anlaby Road.

I was convinced I had wasted the group's time. When I arrived, two other drummers were already set up and ready to go. One was a young girl, the other an older bloke dressed very smartly with a shirt and tie. I tried my best to look really professional when I was setting up, not really knowing what went where on the kit (it had never been out of our flat before). Thankfully I was last on, which also gave me the advantage of being able to get a preview of what I might be asked to play.

As it turned out, two of the audition songs were by a new group called The Kinks: 'You Really Got Me' and 'All Day and All of the Night'. Both were established favourites from my *Beano* annual repertoire. The Gonx's lead singer Dave Gardner announced at the end that they'd chosen me, though this decision might have had less to do with my ability and experience and more that I had a brand-new drum kit, and, with my long hair, didn't look unlike the rest of the group.

So, by November 1964, I had finally arrived, joining Dave Gardner, Steve Powell (bass guitar and vocals) and John Rowe (guitar) in my first band.

Within a couple of weeks – on 10 December 1964, to be exact – I played my first real gig. A double-header too! First a children's party at the Regal Rooms, to be known in the future as the ABC Cinema, and the same building where I saw the Beatles, Mary Wells, The Ronettes and The Kinks. Later that night, we appeared at the Kontiki Club, my old stomping ground (see Appendix 2).

The week after that was even better when we appeared on the same bill as The Aces, 5-Trax and The Hollies at Beverley Road

The Gonx – on the steps in Scarborough. Back row, L-R
Steve Powell, Dave Carmichael, John Rowe. Front row, L-R
Dave Gardner, John Cambridge

Baths. Bobby Elliot, the Hollies' drummer, was another one of my
idols and I took his drum key as a souvenir. Years later, I thought
I would give him a nice surprise and guiltily tried to return it to
him when The Hollies played Hull City Hall – but I was refused
backstage access by their tour manager and therefore still have it in
my possession. I'm sure I'll get it back to him someday.

The Gonx had a regular booking for the Regal Ballroom in
Beverley, which was not only a music venue with a ballroom dance
area but a part-time cinema too. On Fridays and Saturdays there
would be three live bands each evening. Among the many local
musicians I met at the Beverley Regal was Mick Ronson, who also
headlined there regularly with one of the best groups on the scene
at the time, The Crestas. Even then Mick was considered one of the
venue's star performers.

Another great coup for the autograph collection in the early
'60s was the Beatles. They played four times in Hull in total: at

Meet the Gonx. Left to right in this new picture of the up-and-coming Hull group are Steve Hall, John Cambridge, John Rowe, Dave Carmichael and Dave Gardner.

GONX HAVE THINGS TAPED—THEY HOPE!

GO...GO...GO... with the Gonx. They're a Hull group in big demand right at the moment, and seem to spend more time playing out of Hull than they do in it.

Never mind, it's all good business—for the lads, that is.

They've been around for some time now, started off with a true R and B sound which has recently been replaced to some extent by a broader deal, and have collected the laurels wherever they have played.

At the moment, though, they're working out material for a tape to be sent to a London recording company

and hoping that this will give them a chance for stardom which they all say they want and for which they are willing to give up their jobs.

The stage act has also been re-cast. It looks good having more lively and mature.

The Gonx have also been playing with the famous in recent weeks.

Big-name groups like the Four Pennies have played with them. It sounds good, and is good as far as experience goes.

Line-up of the Gonx is: Dave Gardner (vocals), John Cambridge (drums), John Rowe (lead), Dave Carmichael (rhythm), and Steve Hall (bass).

A Gonx newspaper article, c.1965

the Majestic Ballroom on Witham in October 1962 and February 1963, just as they were making it big with 'Love Me Do' and 'Please, Please Me', and then they returned to play at the ABC Cinema, Hull on 24 November 1963 and 16 October 1964, by which time they were massive.

I'm proud to say I was there at the ABC, both times.

The ABC Cinema auditorium had a big raking stalls and cavernous balcony and for the first Beatles' gig there in November 1963 I was upstairs, in the circle and quite a way from the stage. I decided then that when they came back the following year, I would do anything I could to get seats in stalls, even if it meant queuing all night for the privilege.

The box office opened especially early – at midnight in fact – and I managed to get my tickets on the third row, directly in front of John Lennon. On the day they were due to perform, my friend Ricki Dobbs who was also a DJ at the Kontiki Club thought that maybe if we got there early in the afternoon and hung around the stage door, who knows, we might even get their autographs?

So when a Ford Thames van pulled up at the stage door, all covered in graffiti, I thought *Ey up, we're in!* Out stepped all six foot six of Mal Evans, the Beatles' faithful roadie and bodyguard, towering over everybody like a lighthouse with his bright blond hair and dressed in a smart tweed jacket.

Mal was with the Beatles for their whole career, and even appeared in some of their films and played on their records. Apparently

The Beatles – from when John went to see them at the A.B.C in Hull

he hit the anvil with a hammer sound effect on 'Maxwell's Silver Hammer', and sang chorus on 'Yellow Submarine'.

We were half-expecting the Beatles to pile out after him, but unfortunately the van was just full of their equipment and after we'd watched him carry it all in, we followed him across the road to the little café on the first floor of Hammonds (not Picadish, which was on the third floor for those of you who remember), where he ordered a pot of tea and something to eat.

Finally we plucked up courage to approach him, and politely asked if he could he 'get our autograph books signed by the Beatles, please?' He said 'Sure' and put both books in his jacket pocket.

After the show we both waited again for Big Mal to appear to load up the gear and reminded him about our autograph books. 'Oh yes,' he said, 'they're in the dressing room' and off he went to get them.

Now I know that lots of Beatles autographs were supposedly done by Mal, roadies or even on occasion all by George Harrison, so I can't be 100% sure that they are the real deal, but I have compared them to other so-called real examples, and they look pretty close to me.

All the other signatures in my autograph book have the added provenance of having been collected by me, in person. The book includes practically all of the big names in rock music from the '60s and early '70s, including Rod Stewart, the Rolling Stones, The Kinks, The Move, Jeff Beck, Buddy Rich, The Tremeloes, Jimi Hendrix, Tommy Steele, The Small Faces and Manfred Mann.

Anyway, I'll never forget Mal's small 'random act of kindness' that day. He could easily have said 'Too busy'. Whether those autographs are authentic or not, he didn't just tell us to 'piss off' as many probably would have done. He put himself out – and really made one young drummer's day.

Mal was to die tragically when he was shot by police in Los Angeles California in 1976, after the air rifle he was holding was mistaken for a real gun.

Hull in the 1960s offered a rich and varied musical education in my experience, contrary to the unwarranted image of the city as being some sort of cultural Sleepy Hollow. Over the next few years, I was to develop my skills and experience in a number of local bands.

Chapter 2
A GIGGING MUSICIAN

In the summer of 1965, The Gonx continued gigging both locally and further afield. In Scarborough, thanks to a booking from Peter Pitts Management, we played St Peter's Youth Club regularly on Sunday nights. This is where I first met Alan Palmer, lead singer in the group The Mandrakes, who later changed his name to Robert Palmer and went on to have huge hits with 'Addicted to Love', 'Every Kinda People', 'Johnny and Mary' among others, achieving worldwide fame over the next two decades.

We all got on really well and found we had a lot in common musically too. At one stage Alan (Robert), Mick Ronson, Geoff Appleby and myself even considered starting a new band together – a 'super group'. That might seem a bit presumptuous now, considering we were all then unknowns, but given what we all went on to do in the music business, it might have been a very interesting prospect.

We even had a secret rehearsal at a church hall in Scarborough which made me a bit uncomfortable, because I was still in another band at the time and Mick and Geoff were still in The Rats. Obviously Benny Marshall, The Rats' vocalist at the time, would have been devastated if the others had dumped him for an unknown like Robert Palmer.

I remember enjoying learning Palmer's thumping, heavy rock arrangement of the Beatles' 'Eleanor Rigby'. This arrangement was to influence and inspire my attempt with Mick to write our own song, 'The Rise and Fall of Bernie Gripplestone', sometime later. It's a pity that the line-up for the Robert Palmer band never materialised, as he was full of brilliant ideas and did a fantastic job on the arrangement of the song. He was obviously destined for much bigger things.

In his book *Spider from Mars*, Woody Woodmansey also mentions a project he was involved in with Robert Palmer – but seeing as our rehearsals took place a couple of years earlier, it must have been a different project altogether.

In the 1960s the Skyline Ballroom had the reputation of being one of the premier live music venues in Yorkshire, hosting some of the biggest names in the business. It was there, on 16 September 1965, that The Gonx supported The Four Pennies who recently had a hit with 'Juliet'. At that time, the Skyline occupied the whole of the top floor of the Co-op department store. When the store closed in the 1970s so did the ballroom, but it then reopened as Bailey's nightclub, with British Home Stores occupying the former department store. Bailey's remained an active part of Hull nightlife until 1991, when a big drugs bust finally forced it to close its doors. I remember it best as a ballroom and music and dance venue, which was also where some of the best bands of the '60s played.

It was here that I managed, over time, to add many other prestigious names to the autograph book, including Jimi Hendrix – who was very friendly, relaxed and happy to chat to young hopefuls like us before his gig.

Artists who appeared there in the '60s and early '70s include some of the top international bands of the time as well as up-and-comers still cutting their teeth on the live scene. Jimi Hendrix, The Move, Cream, The Troggs and The Small Faces were just some of the acts I saw both as a punter and as drummer in the support act.

I remember one particular evening in early 1966, when I was playing for the Hullabaloos with Mick Wayne on lead guitar. (Mick, you may remember, performed the famous solo on 'Space Oddity'.) We'd heard that John Mayall & the Bluesbreakers were to appear at Skyline, featuring Eric Clapton, who Mick knew from his London days. So Mick and I headed to the ballroom in the afternoon to see if we could catch up with the band after the soundcheck.

I know it might sound unbelievable nowadays, but we didn't see any security: it was as if we were just going shopping. The building was first and foremost a huge department store, after all, and we just went up to the ballroom in the store's lift. Sure enough, the band were on the corner stage, running through a few things as we arrived. When they finished, Mick went over to his buddy Eric to say hello and before long the conversation had turned to guitars and guitarists. I just stood at the side listening intently, but I then heard Mick say to Eric, 'Yeah, but Jimmy's still the governor, isn't he?' Eric replied, 'Oh yes, definitely.'

It turned out that the Jimmy they were referring to was none other than Jimmy Page, still a virtual unknown at the time but also another friend and songwriting collaborator of Mick's. Less than two years later, of course, Led Zeppelin were one of the biggest rock names on the planet.

It was while I was in The Rats that we supported The Move at The Skyline in 1968. I had already seen them play there the year before, and it was their versions of 'So You Want To Be a Rock 'n' Roll Star' (originally by The Byrds) and 'Hey Grandma' (Moby Grape) that I persuaded The Rats to cover in our set, mainly to get away from the usual 12-bar blues stuff that we played. I also remember The Move doing a number with a really catchy 'Ooh, Ooh, Ah, Ah' chorus that night. In the dressing room afterwards, I asked Roy Wood what it was called and was really surprised when he told me it was a number by Gladys Knight & the Pips called 'Stop and Get a Hold of Myself'.

I don't need to remind you that there was no such thing as Google or Amazon in those days, so what was a boy to do? Make enquiries at the local record stores, Hammonds and Sydney Scarborough, to find it was on an LP called *An Album Full of Soul*, which they ordered for me. I suggested to The Rats that they added this to their repertoire too, which they duly did. I looked on it much as the big Liverpool groups did when LPs were brought to the docks by merchant seamen and tracks like 'Twist and Shout', 'Please Mr Postman' and 'Money' became a part of their sets.

'Stop and Get a Hold of Myself' became a very popular addition to The Rats repertoire and we even recorded it during 'The Rise and Fall of Bernie Gripplestone' sessions.

Hardly anybody had heard most of these songs and many punters thought that the groups who played them had actually composed them too. I suppose all of this came about because of the Skyline Ballroom, which was in many ways Hull's window on the musical world.

This was the kind of quality of musical education we experienced in the '60s, when it was much easier, especially as a musician, to get closer to your idols. 'Security' was a much more relaxed concept and bands were all so much more approachable and inclined to do smaller venue gigs in theatres and cinemas. Besides, there were very few arena-sized venues.

I suppose if anybody were to put together a family tree or a timeline of David Bowie's career and all the different groups and individuals who contributed to it, the next stages of my career might figure in an important way.

On 21 August of that same year, 1965, The Gonx won the Locarno Ballroom Beat Group competition and at the same time began getting bookings for bigger venues, albeit still as a support act for better known groups.

But by 4 December, The Gonx had begun to run out of steam and played their last gig at Beverley Youth Centre. Within a couple of weeks, I briefly joined another local group called Attack, formed mostly from the remnants of The Gonx.

In February 1966, after just two months of gigging, I replied to an anonymous advert in the local paper for a 'professional group seeking a drummer'.

The group turned out to be a Hull group called The Hullabaloos, formerly Ricky Knight and The Crusaders, who were managed by John Chichester Constable. Constable was the local aristocrat and lived at the stately home Burton Constable Hall, which was where I successfully auditioned for the band.

The Hullabaloos had already enjoyed huge international success with a cover of Buddy Holly's 'I'm Gonna Love You Too' and were massive in America but not really known here. Their lead singer had recently been replaced by Mick Wayne, the London singer-guitarist who had a song-writing contract with Jimmy Page.

I rehearsed with The Hullabaloos at Burton Constable Hall and our first gig should have been a month-long residency at the Club du Pont de Limay, in Yvelines just east of Paris. I would be paid £8 (an absolute fortune at the time), just to play on Saturday evening and Sunday afternoon. To cut a long story short, though, I was refused permission to play because at 16 years old I was considered to be underage for a work permit. I still have the contracts from

'West One Entertainments Ltd, 20 Manchester Square, London' – another place often connected with David Bowie, who once lived in a flat around there too.

During my time with The Hullabaloos, I became really friendly with Mick who, despite the group's success in the States, was on the bones of his arse in this country as a professional musician.

I remember going round to Mick's West Hull flat once and finding myself in something a bit like Monty Python's 'Four Yorkshiremen' sketch.

'Would you like a cup of coffee, John?'

'Yes please, Mick.'

'Ah, I've no milk, sorry, you'll have to have it black.'

'That's okay.'

'Oh. I've no sugar either.'

'Never mind.'

'… or coffee!'

I ended up with just a cup of hot water.

(Just try telling the kids of today that; they won't believe you!)

Mick had a pipe and unbeknown to me smoked cannabis in it. One day in conversation he asked, 'Is there anywhere round here where I can score?'

'You want to play football?' I replied. 'I play in a team. I can probably get you a game.'

Mick later said he quickly changed the subject when he realised that I didn't have a clue he was sounding me out about the local drug scene!

His bedsit wasn't far from me in Albert Avenue, but as he was obviously struggling to afford even a jar of coffee, my mam and dad, out of pity, would invite him back occasionally for a 'decent meal' after rehearsals. By now my brother Ken had moved out which eventually led to Mick moving in with us – rent-free of course.

Mick's stay with us didn't last long, though: on 30 April 1966, The Hullabaloos played their last ever gig at the Spa Ballroom in Scarborough. I've still got the poster, which Mick signed. He thanked my parents for everything, promising he wouldn't forget all we'd done for him (he didn't). But, for now, I bade him a fond farewell as he headed off in a different musical direction – and, fortunately for him, to much bigger things.

In just three years he would play lead guitar on David Bowie's first hit single 'Space Oddity', (which might also give you a clue how my own connections to Bowie and London were forged).

It was actually Steve Marriott of The Small Faces who suggested 'ABC' as the name for my next band. (I was chatting to Steve after a gig and he suggested, 'Why don't you call yourselves ABC?' I said, 'Why ABC?' and he replied, 'Because it's fucking everywhere – it's free publicity!')

I joined in September 1966, which was also the cue to upgrade my drum kit to a Ludwig (like Ringo Starr), which I have used right through my career up to the present day (boy, they've seen some action!).

ABC mostly gigged around Yorkshire and the North in 1966–7 and supported some quite impressive future legends, including The Searchers, The Fortunes, Family, Zoot Money, Geno Washington, Pink Floyd (yes, that Pink Floyd!), Manfred Mann, The Small Faces and Alan Price.

ABC 1966, L-R John Rowe, Rick Hebblethwaite, John Cambridge, Les Nicol, Steve Powell

ABC 1967 (Mark 2) L-R John Cambridge, Les Nicol, Mike Tyson, Rick Hebblethwaite

It was also while I was in ABC that I first started doing gigs on the same bill as another top Hull band, The Rats. The Rats, now with Mick Ronson, were securing their reputation as the premier group in Hull and were producing the kind of heavy guitar-rock sound that David Bowie sought for the *Man Who Sold the World* and *Ziggy* albums.

Our guitarist in ABC was another local lad, Les Nicol, who was definitely Mick Ronson's guitar gunslinging rival at the time. Les would himself go on to work with some quite notable names, including Leo Sayer, touring and recording with him.

Mick and Les would often trade riffs and tips in Hammonds Music Department on work-free Saturday afternoons. Hammonds was managed by Steeleye Span's Rick Kemp, and I remember Les showing Mick Eric Clapton's solo in 'I Feel Free', which he had already mastered, and which Mick at the time was keen to learn. It was a place in Hull city centre where musicians would often meet to try out new gear and exchange banter. The 'I Feel Free' track was eventually covered by Bowie and the Spiders too, who occasionally performed it live on the Ziggy tours. The Rats' version of this was

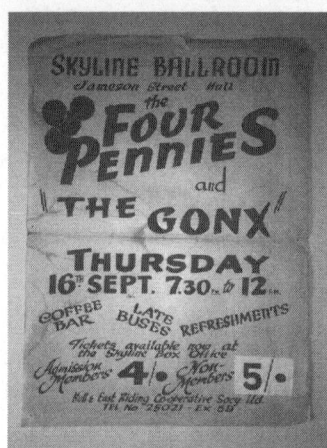
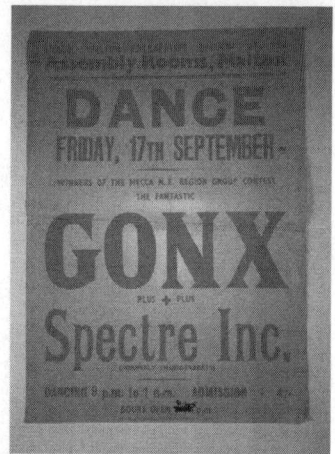
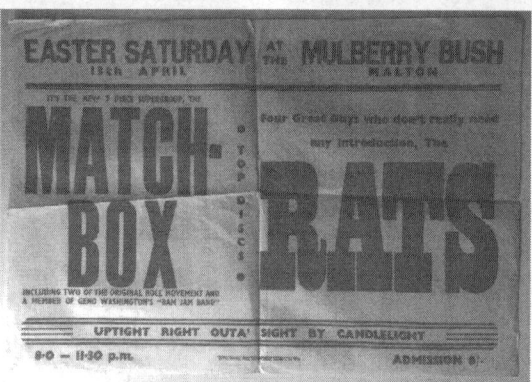
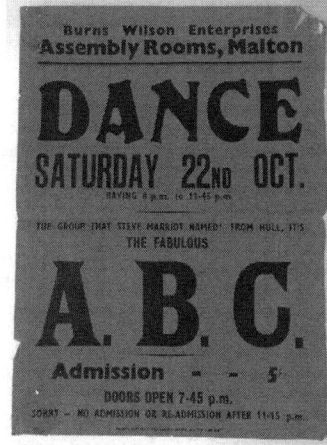

Gig posters: The Gonx at Skyline 1965, The Gonx at Malton 1965, The Rats 1968, ABC 1965, Hullaballoos at Spa 1965 (signed by Mick Wayne)

recorded at Mick's Memorial Concert at the Hammersmith Odeon in 1994, the only time we ever did.

I initially turned an offer to join The Rats down when Jim Simpson, the original Rats' drummer, was about to leave and Mick asked me to cover for some gigs at a very dodgy club in Rouen. Finally, in the autumn of 1967, when Jim's replacement, Clive 'Spud' Taylor, left I succumbed and joined The Rats. Clive and I have stayed good mates over the years and he and his wife Judith are godparents to our youngest daughter, Lucy. It was through joining The Rats that I really got to know Mick Ronson well.

As you can imagine, there are so many rock and roll stories, some now urban myths, about The Rats and Mick, who would go on to become a rock legend himself and record producer.

There were hundreds of venues for live bands in the mid '60s in the Hull and East Yorkshire area: pubs, working men's clubs, ballrooms like the Skyline and the Regal, cinemas, village halls and Beat clubs like the Kontiki and the Gondola. At weekends, young people flocked to them to see live entertainment, drink and to dance. There was plenty of work for a decent outfit, and The Rats had the reputation of being one of the best.

On Friday, 20 October 1967, at The Purple Onion Club in Cleethorpes I made my first outing with The Rats. Once I started to play regularly with them, I rewarded myself with another piece of kit, a Ginger Baker double bass drum, which made its first outing at the Purple Onion Club on 15 May 1968.

The line-up for The Rats had often changed over the years, but when I joined it was Mick Ronson on guitar, Benny Marshall on vocals, Geoff Appleby on bass (soon to be replaced by Keith 'Ched' Cheesman) and me on drums. Contrary to some accounts, Trevor Bolder never played with The Rats, though he did actually join Treacle on stage for one gig when he stood in for Geoff Appleby. I even have a note of the exact date – it was on Wednesday, 24 July 1968.

On that day we were playing Elizabethan Hall (Greatfield High School) billed as Treacle (the name was inspired by Marmalade, a very successful '60s band at the time) and Geoff kept getting an unexplained electric shock from his bass guitar. Only Geoff, nobody else! We tried checking plugs, leads and connections and all had a go

John in full mid-60s posing gear in 1968 (Treacle). Clothes from Carnaby Street, from Don Lill, Treacle's manager

on his guitar, but we couldn't find the cause. At that point, Trevor Bolder, who had turned up early (to be in the audience) and who also knew all of our stuff, stepped in, but he was never a full-time member.

I first got to meet Mick Ronson when he played in The Crestas, and we'd chat in bars before and after gigs. We hadn't really played together, apart from the secret rehearsal with Alan Palmer which came to nothing.

Mick was an all-round musician. He was not just a dedicated and expert guitarist, he was a multi-instrumentalist. One of his big strengths was his knowledge of musical theory which included being able to play classical instruments like piano, cello and violin. This helped him later in his career to be able to score brilliant orchestral arrangements, as would be seen on classic Bowie tracks like 'Life on Mars?' and Lou Reed's 'Perfect Day', though I only ever saw him play guitar when in The Rats.

TREACLE

Manager:
D. LILL, 11 REGINA CRESCENT, VICTORIA AVENUE, HULL
Tel: 42042

Treacle. The Rats, briefly, by another name

Mick had already been stung in a couple of bands in London, including The Voice (a weird, religious cult), and had been seriously ripped off, half-starved and fleeced of all his money. By the time I worked with him in The Rats he was ultra-cautious: the chance of a musical career wasn't enough to have him risk another move away from Hull to anywhere he might fallback into debt.

Without a doubt he was the best guitarist in East Yorkshire at the time, a real showman, definitely ambitious and always wanting to improve – both in terms of how he appeared on stage and the quality of what he was playing. We had a lot in common, I suppose. I just wanted to be the best drummer I could be, and in The Rats we both had the chance to play some great rock and roll music to a big, supportive following around Hull and Yorkshire. At the time neither of us had any idea how far it would take us.

I remember Mick saying to me just after I joined The Rats: 'I've always been in a band with good drummers' which I thought was a really nice compliment, so I replied: 'I've always been in a band with good guitarists … but I'll make an exception with you.'

I'm not certain he realised I was joking.

On 28 October 1967, early on during my time in the band, we were playing Sheffield University and Mick was having a drunken argument backstage with Chris Farlowe (who'd had a hit with the Rolling Stones' 'Out of Time') about who was the best guitarist: Jeff Beck (Mick's absolute hero) or Chris's then guitarist, the phenomenal Albert Lee?

Now at the time Ronno didn't drink very often, and he wasn't great at handling it when he did. So after just one Black Velvet (Guinness and Cider, the poor man's Black Velvet; Guinness and Champagne is the rich man's), believe me, he was steaming

I remember him being in hysterics just at Albert's name, which was considered very old-fashioned at the time.

'You can't be a rock guitarist and be called *Albert*,' he said (loudly and within Albert Lee's hearing) and then collapsed laughing. 'It's a grandad name!'

This was also the same night Mick dressed up as Batman's sidekick Robin, complete with wellies, to go on stage.

I don't think any of us were ever starstruck by the many famous people we played alongside. Certainly Mick wasn't overawed by Albert Lee, or even a group like The Small Faces, who we must have played with at least four times. And some of the headline acts we supported were going to go on and make it really big – though at the time we were only the same as them, I suppose; musicians trying to scratch a living doing what we loved best. We all listened to the same groups, played many of the same venues and knew lots of the same people.

But they do say you should never meet your idols, and I remember when Mick finally came face to face with his hero.

On Sunday, 17 March 1968 we were on the same bill as Jeff Beck at the Cat Ballou Club in Grantham. As you can probably imagine, Mick was in his absolute element. He not only idolised

Jeff Beck, he wanted to be Jeff Beck. Later he even bought his Gibson Les Paul guitar because that was what Jeff Beck played. Just take a look at the typical Rats set list, it's nearly all Jeff Beck! (See Appendix 3).

And now he was about to finally meet his idol, in the flesh. How would he react?

The Jeff Beck Band's vocalist at that time was none other than an up-and-coming singer called Rod Stewart. Contrary to some accounts, his normal bass player (Ronnie Wood) did *not* play for him that night (somebody called Junior stood in) and his drummer was Micky Waller. How do I remember all this? You've guessed it, I got their autographs, not in the book this time but on the back of an empty guitar string packet.

When The Rats had played their set, we came off stage into the shared dressing room, where Rod was now wandering around in jeans and a striped rugby shirt, singing his heart out and doing vocal warm-ups, oblivious to everyone. Meanwhile, in the other corner, Jeff was tuning up his Les Paul and had his ear to the neck trying to hear the unamplified strings (these being the days when practice amps and electric guitar tuners were yet to be invented). There were a few nods and 'How are you doing' and 'Alright, lads' as we came in, but the rest of The Rats and I were all watching Mick out the corner of our eye, eager to see how he would behave, more than anything.

Mick just casually walked past him, coolly nodded and put his guitar in his case. We could only guess what was going on inside his head. *Would he do his normal big friendly handshake*, we wondered.

Or was he about to jump on Jeff and give him a love bite?

After a few minutes he finally plucked up enough courage to sit next to his hero and watch Jeff as he tuned up ready to play his guitar.

There was one tune in particular which Jeff Beck played in his set, a real show-off party piece. It was 'Guitar Boogie', an instrumental originally by Chuck Berry, which Jeff had rechristened 'Jeff's Boogie', involving lots of tricky hammering-on and pulling-off. Anyway, Mick (who, remember, wanted to be Jeff Beck) was desperately trying to master it.

'Could you just, er, show me that bit in "Jeff's Boogie", please, Jeff. I think it's the third riff in, if you don't mind, please,' he finally asked. His nose was virtually pressed to Jeff's fretboard in the dressing room as Jeff demonstrated the particularly tricky 'third riff in'.

'Er, sorry. Could you just show me again, a bit slower, please,' he asked, as Jeff repeated the 'tricky bit' as slowly as he could.

'Er, sorry, Jeff, could you just show me that bit just once again please, a bit slower,' Mick asked again.

'Fucking hell,' said Beck. 'Any slower an' I'll fucking stop.'

I think Mick got the message and just left it there.

We had a reel-to-reel tape recorder with us that night and recorded all of the Jeff Beck Group's set. They were playing songs from his up-and-coming album *Truth*, so as soon as we got back home to rehearsals we practically learned the whole album. Other local bands were amazed that we could play all of these songs from an album which wasn't released until July 1968, four months later.

Unfortunately, nobody knows what happened to that recording – at least, not so far.

When Mick did finally master 'Jeff's Boogie', it became his showcase guitar solo instrumental, and one which was always included in The Rats' live set, re-rechristened 'Mick's Boogie' (now that he had finally become Jeff Beck).

I'd been there with Mick when he collected his Les Paul guitar from Pat Cornell's music shop on Spring Bank, near to Hull town centre, in 1968. He had been gardening for the council during the day (his 'proper', daytime job was as a groundsman, cutting grass, marking out sports pitches and carrying out other municipal gardening work). Ian 'Taffy' Evans, the roadie who often drove us to nearly all our gigs, picked us all up for an evening gig in Cleethorpes, collecting Mick around 4.30 as he finished, to get him to Cornell's before it closed.

Pat Cornell had already phoned Mick to tell him his guitar had arrived, so he just went in, opened the case, and didn't even get it out to try. He just passed over his Fender Telecaster in part-exchange before jumping back in the van. He played the new Les Paul that night too, without adjusting the action or anything.

If you look at early Rats' photos, you can see the guitar was still black, as he hadn't yet gone to all the lengths of stripping it so that it was 'blond' (like him). Mick was a real perfectionist when it came to music and would do anything to get a better sound on his guitar.

Somebody must have told him that stripping the black lacquer off would improve its tone – but I've been told by other guitarists that where this might work for an acoustic guitar, it would make very little difference on a solid body electric guitar, and only really change the way it looked.

That particular guitar was to become forever associated with Mick, and all those great *Ziggy* albums in particular. Mick, who was never brilliant at managing his money, told me, just before he died, that he had given it away to a Hard Rock Café in New York. Later it somehow appeared in Melbourne, Australia, where it was rescued by Rick Tedesco and taken back to his Guitar Hangar store in Connecticut USA.

I heard that the same guitar was later bought by a very wealthy Bowie memorabilia collector for a life-changing amount of money and is now safely locked away in a tax haven (Monaco), a long, long way from Spring Bank. It certainly is a well-travelled instrument.

Around the late '60s, it seemed that all of the bands in Hull had at least one roadie, someone who would also drive the band and their gear and hump some of the heavy items upstairs and into the venue, ready to set up and sound-check. The Rats regularly had several roadies, all eager to carry in our gear at gigs, which usually meant they would get free entry as a result. Most bands' gig vans were fairly small affairs, Ford Thames or Commers, and nothing like the luxurious modern Camper vans people go away in nowadays.

The Rats' new gig van was to be a former Needler's Chocolate Delivery Wagon, which they were selling off, cheap! Basically there was just one door at the back and shelves on either side for chocolate products – which actually turned out to be very useful for our purposes. With a few quick alterations, these were easily converted into bunks, where we could even have a lie-down on our way to or from gigs.

In August 1968, rather than let the van sit idle all week between gigs, four of us decided to use ours as a kind of poor man's camper van and have a summer holiday.

All of the band were asked if they fancied going on a holiday in the van but Jeff Appleby and Benny declined so Chris Adamson and Eric (our roadies), Mick Ronson and I met to decide where to go.

It was unanimous: 'Seaside!'

Once that had been decided, we started to look at which seaside we would go to and Chris, who was going to be the one driving, came up with the idea of Yarmouth. I think this must have been in the days when Yarmouth wasn't even 'Great' because the route to get there, especially from Hull, was a real trek. Even today the roads to Yarmouth are really slow. Leaving Hull you can get stuck behind a tractor, which is stuck behind a JCB, which is stuck behind a combine harvester and a steam roller – and that's before you've even got to the Humber Bridge. It was even worse then!

Do you remember the 1963 film *Summer Holiday* with Cliff Richard and the Shadows? Maybe not, so here's a recap: guess what, they all go on a summer holiday on a double-decker bus, with 'no more working for a week or two'. It was actually filmed in Greece and everybody looks tanned, clean-shaven and healthy, there are beautiful blue seas, and the weather is glorious, sunny and with cloudless clear skies. Every so often they all burst into song, instruments appear from nowhere and, surprise, surprise, Cliff gets the girl in the end.

Well, this was The Rats, from Hull – and Yarmouth was nothing like that!

The Rats on holiday going swimming! Summer of 1968. L-R Mick Ronson, Eric McMinn, Chris Adamson, John Cambridge

Once we'd navigated our way there, we had to decide where to stay. Nowadays you'd have to find a special car park and there would be facilities where you'd pay to get a wash or a shower and go to the toilet. In those days, there weren't even double yellow lines or parking meters, so we just pulled up, literally straight onto the sea front.

There were no facilities in the van, either. It was basically like a big tent on wheels, so we made sure we parked near some swimming baths with a toilet nearby. Sometimes we didn't bother with a shower and improvised with a soapy rub-down and a dip in the swimming pool. I'm pretty sure some of the lads didn't bother with the toilet either, and improvised in the pool just the same. It's a good job those stories about chemicals in swimming pools reacting with your pee to change colour and catch you out weren't true, or it might have looked like a Red Arrows Display Team in there.

We'd all only left school a few years before, so our daily routine was probably what you'd expect from a group of single young lads out to enjoy themselves. A lot of our daytimes were spent in the amusements and the funfair, where Mick especially would spend hours on the bingo and one-armed bandits, putting back every penny he'd won as he played.

After three days or so of this, I suggested that we do something different, maybe go into town and do a bit of exploring, see some of the shops. As we were walking into town, I noticed two elderly, Romany-type ladies coming towards us down the main shopping street.

'Buy some heather? Lucky white heather?' I heard them say.

Both women were obviously the real McCoy, in long flowing dresses, bandanas and cardigans, with big dangly earrings and so on – and Ronno made a beeline for them. The rest of us wondered first of all what he was going to say to them and then whether or not he was 'on the pull'.

'Do you read palms as well?' he asked. 'Tell fortunes?'

To which one of the ladies answered straightaway, 'Yes, of course.'

If he'd asked if she could plaster a ceiling or lay a patio, I think she'd have answered 'yes' –as long as they had their palms crossed with some of Mick's silver.

So, all the time I'm waiting by his side, thinking *What a bloody waste of money!* while she's telling him this and that, most of which I couldn't hear properly. When he finally finished, I said: 'Right, are we going then?', but one of the ladies pointed a bony finger at me.

'Would you like your palm reading?' she said.

'Oh, no thank you, I'm alright,' I replied, but Mick gave me a big dig in the ribs.

'Gooo on!' he said, and all I could think when I handed over my half-crown was *That's this morning's bacon sandwich gone.*

She held my hand and began to speak. I wasn't really paying much attention until the very last thing she said, which made my ears prick up.

'Do you have anything to do with music?' she asked.

'Why do you say that?' I said, still not wanting to give anything away.

'You're going to have a very successful career in music,' she said.

'Oh really?' I said. 'Well, thank you.' And at that I started to leave.

Mick had been watching all of this, beady-eyed, over my shoulder, so I should have expected what he did next. He thrust his hand in front of her and said: 'Did you see anything about music on mine?'

She never even glanced at Mick's palm again. She just looked him in the eye. There was a short pause before she just said …

'No.'

I often wonder if she just got us mixed up; after all, she did look a bit cross-eyed.

* * *

The Rats' main roadies at this time were Ian 'Taffy' Evans, Chris Adamson, Peter 'Muff' Mirfin and Stuey George. Pete was the mechanic who serviced Bowie's Rover car for him when he came to stay in Hull.

Stuey George was a doorman at the Halfway House on Spring Bank, and used to help us out as a roadie and driver. I can't remember Halfway being a particularly rough pub (which might have had something to do with Stuey's presence!). That honour was reserved for the likes of Rayner's on Hessle Road, where you'd often see the 'three-day millionaire' trawlermen out splashing the cash, drinking and getting into brawls when they were home on shore leave.

By ten o'clock, with a few bevvies in them, things could turn nasty in some places and you definitely needed somebody fearless like Stuey to be able to sort things out!

He was a real character and was always useful to have around in case of trouble. Stuey had earned a well-deserved local reputation for being a hard case and wouldn't suffer fools gladly, so he also acted as our minder as well as being our friend. We still keep in touch, and I've known him now for over 50 years.

I remember pranking him one night (Saturday, 20 January 1968) after a Rats' gig at the King's Manor, a tourist attraction in York and a part of York University. Originally the King's Manor was the Abbot's House of St Mary's Abbey, circa 1270, and is a Grade I listed building, so you can imagine how spooky it might look, especially at night. (If you can't, just have a look on Google Earth.)

We set up all the gear in the concert room, did the usual checks and found out what time we were going on. With a bit of time on our hands we decided to explore the grounds and find out where the nearest pub was. Mick, Benny and myself ventured out into the huge dark courtyard, which was really dark now, and headed to the stone entrance where there was some sort of cloister running across the opening and where you could get through to the front.

As we were passing through, we noticed that there was a long corridor going right across the courtyard and that the only light came in through the stained glass windows. It was the ideal place to have a pee instead of traipsing all the way back into the venue – and so we did.

This is when I got the idea.

At the end of the corridor, you could just make out a big, old, wooden door, set about a foot into the end wall. It looked very spooky and I decided I would get one of the white sheets I wrapped my drums in before I put them in their cases and become a ghost.

I went back through the big double door at the end to get the biggest sheet, put it over my head and waited. Benny then rushed back in and said to Stuey, 'I think there's a bit of bother outside, Stu, you'd better come.'

Stuey being the kind of person he is (afraid of no man) rushed outside (the whole band were in on it by now), ready for whatever was kicking off. By the time he gets outside there's nobody around, so Benny walks back down the corridor with him with the others following.

'They must have gone, Stu,' said Benny, 'Ey, I'm busting for a piss now, though.'

So the rest of The Rats, with Stuey standing at the end, stopped to pee against this wall. Meanwhile I was waiting with a white sheet covering me from head to toe standing nearest to him.

'Ey, this is just like Tom Brown's Schooldays in here, innit?' I heard Stuey say as I took a step closer to him, slowly at first, but still covered by the sheet.

Then I took another step, still covered. Then another!

I could see, even through this sheet, that Stuey was looking me up and down as he was peeing against the wall when suddenly – bang! – he's off like a shot (I don't think he'd even zipped up), legging it back to the safety of the Manor.

The Rats at The Duke of Cumberland Pub in Ferriby 1968 –
John Cambridge, Benny Marshall, Ched Cheesman, Mick Ronson

'I knew you buggers were having me on all along,' he said later. At the time we weren't convinced; Stuey had rushed back to the venue, passing everyone he was there to protect, at world record speed.

Stuey, like Ronno, loved playing the one-armed bandits. One night we had stopped at the famous Norman's Café at Kilpin near Howden, which was a bit like the Blue Boar at Watford Gap where many musicians stopped for a coffee break as they were nearing Hertfordshire and London. Stuey and Ronno had agreed to go shares at Norman's and Mick had been pumping tanners into one slot machine until he finally ran out, coming away with nothing. When Stuey started playing it, he dropped the jackpot almost straight away but then had no intention of sharing it!

Well, Ronno had a bit of a sulk on as Stuey began scooping his winnings into his pockets, most of which Ronno had fed into the machine himself. 'I thought we were sharing,' he said. 'I don't remember saying that,' said Stuey, though he did buy Ronno a packet of fags as a consolation.

Mick slung them right back, telling him he could 'shove 'em up his arse'!

Stuey ended up joining Mick and the others in London and became David Bowie's bodyguard for years, another of Mick's recruits. He even went to Switzerland with Bowie, and set up his own security company. He could no doubt write his own memoirs, which would make a *very* interesting book, considering all he must have seen.

The 60s' 'beat' scene really began to take off from 1963 with groups like The Hollies, Gerry & The Pacemakers, Brian Poole and The Tremeloes and, of course, the Beatles. But the advantage the Beatles had over all of these big groups was that apart from having early hit records with cover versions of songs like 'Twist and Shout', they composed nearly all of their own material.

As you can see by the typical Rats' set (Appendix 3), our playlist was dominated by heavy rock covers (mostly Mick's idols) and there was no original Rats' material. That's because we had none! There was very little chance of us breaking through by covering other people's songs or by being little more than a Jeff Beck tribute band!

John with Stuart 'Stuey' George

As a Beatles' fan, I loved the fact that Lennon and McCartney were able to come up with all of these original and brilliant songs, and it always inspired me to want to write my own stuff. I still have notebooks, pads and scraps of paper all over the house with lyrics and ideas for songs on them and I even shared with David a fragment of a lyric, which he asked to keep.

People have often asked me if I kept any of his scribbles and early drafts, as they would probably be priceless now! To be honest, David never seemed to write like that. It was as if the song was almost always finished and complete in his head when he played it for the first time. He often used a typewriter to type up the finished lyrics and there were slight alterations, words changed or added, and so on, but it was not a long, drawn-out process, always very quick and complete.

I was only 17 and in ABC when I first suggested to Steve Powell that we have a go at writing a song. We came up with a forgettable little ditty called 'L.S.D.', all about the effects of a certain dangerous hallucinatory drug. I must have thought I could write my own 'Lucy in the Sky with Diamonds', even though I was just a naive young kid who had no experience of taking drugs whatsoever!

How I thought I could write lyrics about something I knew absolutely nothing about still defeats me. As was to be expected, the song never really went anywhere – although a few years ago the British Music Archive asked if they could put it on their website britishmusicarchive.com. I've never listened to it.

I will always think of The Rats as a great live, rock and roll covers band. The line-up of Benny Marshall, Geoff Appleby, Ched Cheesman, Mick Ronson and myself played plenty of loud, heavy rock and roll blues with endless Jeff Beck-style electric guitar solos and harmonica breaks.

I thought it was time we tried to write our own songs. Surely we would have more chance of getting a record deal with original material. Mick Ronson, also hungry for fame, agreed, so one night I picked him up from his mum's on Greatfield Estate and brought him back to the flat in Brisbane Street. I told him I had an idea for a song we could write together, but not a love song with 'moon and June'-style lyrics! It would be something a bit different.

What I really had in mind was something like 'Bike' by Pink Floyd, which somebody on YouTube has described as 'the most insane song ever' (it probably is). We ended up writing 'The Rise and Fall of Bernie Gripplestone', a song all about a coalman. I got the idea for the name 'Bernie Gripplestone' from the John Lennon film *How I Won the War* and his character Bernard Gripweed. The 'rise and fall' part came from The Shadows' 'Rise and Fall of Flingel Bunt', and as for the musical arrangement, Mick said he also nicked a bit of 'Eleanor Rigby' for the middle eight sequence.

We recorded this in Keith Herd's makeshift front-room studio – before he'd built the famous Fairview Studios in Willerby, near Hull. I remember egg boxes on the wall for soundproofing. Mick's 'backward' guitar solo was inspired by the Beatles' experiment with sound on 'Taxman' and 'I'm Only Sleeping', and I remember he and Keith spent a long time recording the solo the 'usual way', before Mick copied and played it backwards in 'normal' time (as near as he could). If you listen to it, try to imagine Keith carefully counting out the beats so Mick wouldn't overrun it on the solo.

The other tracks we recorded were covers of 'Stop and Get a Hold of Myself', 'Morning Dew' and 'Guitar Boogie' (what else?) – all in the same session. I don't remember us ever doing 'Bernie

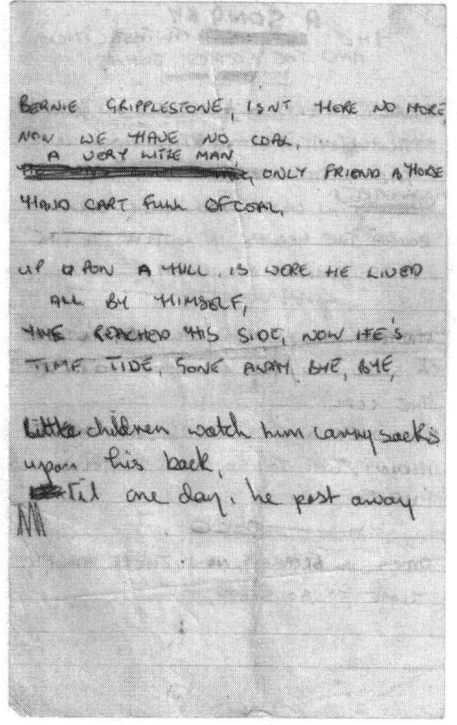

The Rise and Fall of Bernie Gripplestone,
handwritten lyrics

Gripplestone' live, perhaps for obvious reasons. No doubt someone will correct me if I'm wrong!

People have speculated whether the title 'The Rise and Fall Of' might have triggered David's *The Rise and Fall of Ziggy Stardust and the Spiders from Mars*. To be honest, I think that's a bit of a long shot: David's was a completely different concept! But with David you could never really be sure; he would collect ideas for tunes or lyrics from everywhere and then add some magic to make them his own.

On Monday, 6 January 1969, I was invited by Mick Wayne to London to watch his new band Junior's Eyes recording at the legendary Trident Studios in St Anne's Court, Soho. I went down on the train and got the Tube right across London to Mick's flat, only to be told he was still at the studio recording (no mobiles in those days). When I finally got there, I had a great night watching them record and eventually stayed the night at his place.

I watched them play live at the famous Klooks Kleek Club in Hampstead the following night and then came back the following day on the train, really grateful that he had taken the trouble to arrange this treat for me. It seemed as if there was more to this than met the eye.

Wednesday, 2 April 1969 marked my final gig with The Rats (for now at least – there were to be other gigs and reunions many years later!) at the Elizabethan Hall School Dance on Greatfield – which was just a stone's throw away from Mick Ronson's home.

For the next couple of days (including Good Friday) we rehearsed at Woodmansey Village Hall – again, all day! On Saturday I was playing football and anyway, by this time I'd just about had enough. This seemed like rehearsal overload.

But if Mick had his way, there was going to be one every day over the Easter weekend. I had something else on: Angie, who would later become my wife, and I were seeing each other more seriously, so I refused to do another rehearsal on the Sunday as well.

Sadly, nobody in the band had the decency, or guts to actually warn me that this was a sackable offence or even to tell me to my face I was going to be sacked from The Rats. Maybe it had already been decided and whatever I'd said or done would have made no difference. Instead of trying to compromise, maybe to do just evenings, I had a knock on the door from Jim Simpson who had been asked to deputise for me that week. He came round to our house on the Tuesday, holding an envelope with some gig money I was owed and to deliver me the bad news.

And that was that, I was out of The Rats!

I was soon to be replaced by another young keen drummer, waiting in the wings, Mick 'Woody' Woodmansey, ex-drummer with The Roadrunners in Driffield.

For a couple of months after that I contented myself earning a living as an apprentice plasterer with my dad,and playing just on Monday and Tuesday nights with my mate and ex-Rat colleague Geoff Appleby, at his in-laws' pub the Brickmakers Arms on Walton Street, Hull. There we were joined by Eric Lee, formerly of The Aces.

It was mostly a free and easy, a throwaway night – a kind of old-fashioned karaoke with volunteers getting up to do spots. Quite relaxed and a good laugh all the same.

Throughout this time I had still been following the career of my old Hullabaloos' friend Mick Wayne, albeit from a distance, through articles in *Melody Maker*, postcards and the odd phone call from London where he was now based. Mick had been in a couple of bands since The Hullabaloos – The Tickle and Bunch of Fives – and had even released singles with them. But now he was getting a lot of publicity in the music press and airplay on the radio for his new band Junior's Eyes ('You can fool most adults, but you can never pull the wool over Junior's eyes'). Now they were turning out to be Mick's most successful group yet.

Junior's Eyes was the modern equivalent of an underground band, I suppose, but at the end of the 60s they were gaining quite a mainstream reputation, and had played many of the nice clubs around London, a few festivals, John Peel's show and others, and were getting mentions in the national music press. They also had plenty of work on their books.

Out of the blue, Mick called me to say Junior's Eyes would be playing the Penthouse Club in Scarborough on 29 May 1969, and asked: 'Why don't you come along?' It was great to see him again, and we had a good catch-up and natter in the dressing room. As he was about to go on for the second set, he said 'Do you fancy getting up and doing a number with us?' Well, I didn't really, but did anyway! It was near the end of their set and we did 'Rock Me Baby', an old classic we also used to cover in The Rats.

What I didn't realise was that this time I was actually being auditioned to join the band!

I thought Mick had asked me to Trident earlier in the year just because he knew I'd really enjoy it. Maybe, though, he'd been sowing a few seeds.

What I thought had been just a nice get-together and generous gesture by an old mate had actually served as a team bonding session with my future colleagues. Now it seemed like my sacking from The Rats was noy only fortuitous, it was meant to be. A couple of days later, Mick Wayne rang to ask me formally if I'd like to join Junior's Eyes.

Chapter 3
BOWIE AND THE LONDON YEARS

Naturally I said yes to this fantastic offer. Who, at my age and in my position, wouldn't? Going to London to improve your career chances was a no-brainer in those days (even the Beatles had moved there). The big studios, media outlets and all the right people were based there. There was plenty going on and it seemed that all of the best work opportunities for me had come from mixing with people there.

The first thing I had to do was to drive from Hull in my old Hillman Minx, pre-Google Maps and satnav, to a big hippy farmhouse, The Old Rectory Farm, near Scoulton in Norfolk. It was owned by someone called 'Cressida' (I've still got my dad's handwritten directions) and I was going to spend the night of 8 June 1969 sleeping on the couch as I waited for the rest of my new bandmates from Junior's Eyes to arrive.

When they did get there early the following morning, they had a new guitarist with them too. Tim Renwick was an experienced session player and a highly respected guitarist who went on to play with Pink Floyd for 20 years, as well as Eric Clapton, Phil Collins, The Sutherland Brothers and Quiver, and many others.

Tim's a great bloke too, very talented and still in demand today. He has been another lifelong friend. While we were at the farmhouse he told me that he once used to be in a band called Little Women. When I asked him where he got the idea for the name. He said, 'From a drummer in a band who supported us at the Cat Ballou Club in Grantham'.

Dad Cambridge's directions to Scoulton,
Norfolk to meet Junior's Eyes

That drummer was me! Another one of these amazing coincidences in my life.

We began a week of rehearsals, though it seemed strange at first that their old drummer stayed to watch his replacement cut his teeth with the band. My debut gig, on 13 June, was a particularly memorable all-nighter at the University of Sussex in Brighton alongside Free, Bakerloo and The Village.

The next day I headed back to Hull, only for the car to seize up on the M1, so I didn't actually arrive home until 5.40 am. Then I headed back to London on the Tuesday to record a short selection of film music with Junior's Eyes, after which we played the City University, London, followed by Hammersmith College of Art and Design on 21 June.

More London work quickly followed, including my debut on 23 June at the Marquee Club in Soho; then, on 24 June, another all-nighter at Queen's College, Oxford with Pink Floyd, Free and Ten Years After. This was followed by the London Lyceum on the 27.

30 June/1 July saw us in Trident Studios, Soho to record with Junior's Eyes, followed by gigs at the Pavilion in Hemel Hempstead on Friday, 4 July (recorded for John Peel's show), Friday 11 July at The Queen's Hall, Barnstaple and the Racecourse, Nottingham on Saturday 12 July, also with John Peel.

On Sunday, we recorded *The Stuart Henry Radio Show* at the BBC Studios in London and on Monday I returned to Hull, and the day after, I got engaged to Angela. Busy, busy!

I started by dossing at Mick Wayne's flat for a few days before I managed to get a spot at 24 Gloucester Place Mews. I say 'spot' because this was an upmarket mews cottage in the heart of London, W1, a very salubrious part of Marylebone. Just round the corner was the now blue-plaque house where John Lennon had lived the year before.

Tim Renwick, our guitarist, was already staying at the Mews, which belonged to the manager of Blue Cheer, an American group who were billed as 'the loudest band in the world'. (I bet the neighbours were glad we had moved in and not them.) We were basically house-sitting because he was out of the country a lot; in fact, I don't think I ever met him.

Situated on a millionaire's row not far from Oxford Street, Park Lane and Mayfair, it was a very plush apartment – unlike our downstairs 'flat'. This bit downstairs was basically a garage with a staircase connecting to the actual apartment. And that's where we slept, on mattresses on the floor with a curtain dividing the space between us. We did use the upstairs, to cook, use the bathroom, and to chill out. It was really handy for Oxford Street, we regularly visited the Golden Egg (a bit like a Wimpy bar) late at night for syrup pancakes and ice cream.

We had some pretty famous celebrity rock star neighbours, including none other than Alvin Lee, the guitarist in Ten Years After. We met him now and again, although he did occasionally have some musical house-sitters himself, which included Ronnie 'Plonk' Lane, The Faces and, of course, Rod Stewart who would often call around in his bright yellow Marcos sports car, which looked like a yellow Batmobile.

Junior's Eyes, summer of 1969! Taken on a film set somewhere in London.
L-R John Cambridge, Grom Kelly, Tim Renwick, John 'Honk' Lodge and
Mick Wayne

Tim Renwick had the only record player between us and I remember him playing the Beatles' *Abbey Road* and Harry Nilsson's
'Everybody's Talkin' (Echoes)' to death, both of which were recent
releases.

All of the rest of Junior's Eyes smoked dope – and I mean smoked as regularly as my dad lit up his Park Drives. One night they got me to try it, and I puked my guts up. Never again! Whenever they were having one of their sessions (which seemed like always), I'd go to the nearest pub instead and often sit on my own with a pint of Watney's Red Barrel.

We stayed at Gloucester Place until the end of September, then moved to 81, St Helen's Garden W10 – into Flat One (though still only on mattresses) with John 'Honk' Lodge, who was already living there. Roger and I shared one room and Tim had another, while Mick Wayne was nearby down Ladbroke Grove. This made things a lot handier for transport to and from gigs and rehearsing. I finally began to really settle in with Junior's Eyes and to feel like a pro at last.

Being a professional musician in Junior's Eyes also meant travelling a lot and playing new venues both at home and abroad. As the bookings became more and more exotic, we thought nothing of doing stints at venues like the famous Star Club in Hamburg, where the Beatles, as virtual unknowns, had played just seven years before.

Junior's Eyes, London, summer of 1969. L-R John 'Honk' Lodge, John Cambridge, Mick Wayne, Tim Renwick, Grom Kelly

There were lots of other up-and-coming English bands also booked for the club, all keen to follow in the footsteps of the Beatles, and I got to meet some great legends of the future, well before they were famous. We went to Bremen to record for the TV programme *Beat Club*, a live show similar to *Ready, Steady, Go*. On the show with us were Delaney & Bonnie, an American band featuring Eric Clapton, who had just joined them.

I remember enjoying a drink and a chat with Ozzy Osbourne at the bar when he played the Star Club in the band Earth, who later changed their name to Black Sabbath (and recorded a track called 'Junior's Eyes'!). I also had a drink with Jon Anderson from Yes (who like Earth, we were sharing the bill with at the club) and I found out Jon was from the same area of Manchester as my mother.

I met interesting people from all over the world, including the members of the American group Ohio Express who performed at the Star Club with us and who had a big hit with 'Yummy, Yummy, Yummy'. One of the group gave me an original Old Grey Whistle Test badge, which I still have somewhere (not the kind you can now buy through mail order, but the *real deal*).

Back in England Junior's Eyes toured extensively. Following a gig at Mothers in Birmingham, the great Robert Plant came up on to the stage and asked if he and a few of his mates could borrow our equipment to jam.

On 16 July 1969, and just four days before man's first landing on the moon, David Bowie's hit single 'Space Oddity', complete with our guitarist Mick Wayne's wonderful lead solo, started to get serious airplay on the radio and very positive reviews – although it was initially the subject of a BBC embargo of songs connected to the lunar landing.

The producer Tony Visconti initially turned down 'Space Oddity' when David played him the demo, and the legendary producer Gus Dudgeon, who loved the song, did it instead. Tony was then brought in for the album and, on his recommendation, and with David's approval, Mick Wayne and Junior's Eyes were invited to Trident Studio to help record the rest of Bowie's new album, also to be called *David Bowie* (later *Space Oddity*).

Rather than hire a selection of diverse session musicians to play on the album, Bowie and Tony Visconti decided to use a band of compatible musicians to record the rest of the tracks. It also made financial sense to use a band rather than paying higher individual day rates for session musicians.

As David would soon be looking to start a new band himself, in order to play some of these tracks live on stage, this put Junior's Eyes in a very favourable position.

When you start keeping professional company like this, when you share a stage or a dressing room with artists who view you as an equal, it really builds your self-esteem. What's more, my professional experience and maturity was growing fast and I was gaining quite an impressive musical CV! By giving me this opportunity, Mick Wayne had more than paid me back for lodging with us briefly in Hull. I was loving every minute, and the awkward and unpleasant circumstances of my departure from The Rats already seemed a distant memory.

In his book, Woody Woodmansey wrote that he thought I was 'brave' to make the move to London. It set an example, apparently, and opened the door for others! Well, it certainly did for some! I suppose in many respects it had been a bit of a leap of faith, but at this point being 'brave' had definitely paid off and life was good!

I took stock and began to count my blessings:

- I was living in central London, centre of the 1960s' music universe.
- I was finally in a professional band, a full-time musician, with good prospects.
- We had plenty of work on the books, including stints at famous national and international venues.
- We were working with exciting musicians, not just supporting them.
- I was about to begin recording in a top studio with someone who could write hit songs and was obviously going places ....

It seemed as if the clairvoyant sisters from Yarmouth had actually been right – a successful career in music now seemed to lie before me. For a budding, ambitious young drummer, what could have been finer?

More importantly, what could possibly go wrong?

There have been quite a few careless errors made by writers and well-meaning experts about my time with David. I hope to put some of those right,and separate some of the myths and mistakes from the truth of what really happened. In other words, all the hype.

I didn't meet David until a few days before we worked together, and when I did, we instantly got on really well.

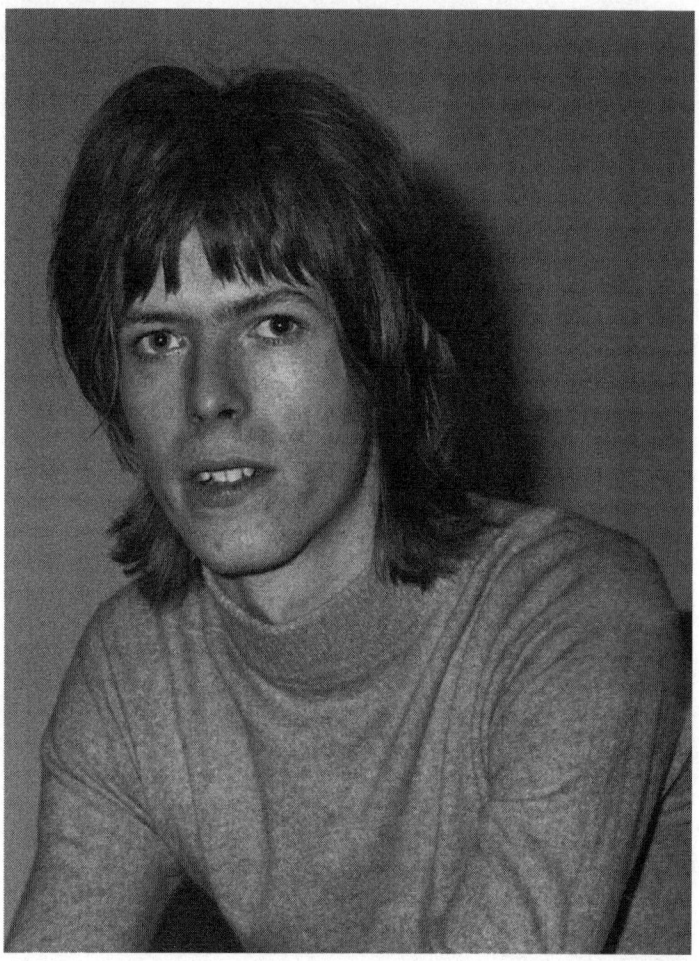

David Bowie in late 1968, about the time that he wrote 'Space Oddity'

That first meeting with David was in early July 1969, just a few days before the official recording sessions, on Wednesday, 16 July 1969. It was Tony Visconti who made the first official introduction between us. This really was just to say hello and to be briefed by him and Bowie prior to going in the studio.

David talked us through the songs. He didn't even play any of them, just talked, and the next time I saw him was in the studio.

David was very slim and curly-haired (I assume this was a perm because his hair was never naturally that curly again at any other point in his career!). Whereas the rest of us typically wore blue denim jeans and T-shirts, he always seemed to prefer bright coloured corduroy trousers, red or turquoise, and knitted jumpers.

Even at the gigs we did at this point, we would often just wear on stage the same ordinary clothes that we'd arrived in. The dressing up didn't really start until we did the first Hype glam rock concert some months later – Mr Fish dresses and a fancy Japanese wardrobe certainly weren't a part of David's stage wear at this point!

I could see straightaway that David had a really good sense of humour. He was clearly a very intelligent man and could talk knowledgably about almost anything, it seemed, and to anyone, whether duke or dustman. He always had something interesting or relevant to say.

* * *

In the time I knew them, David and Angie never seemed to me to be a lovie-dovie couple. However, Tony Visconti writes in his book about their soppy behaviour and nicknames for each other – like 'Davie Wavie' and 'Angie Pangie'. David would never smother her and say 'give us a kiss' as many young courting couples might do. It always seemed to be Angie who was the pushy one, and she was certainly more touchy-feely with him than he ever was with her.

Angie was full of personality, very confident and always larger than life. You would often hear Angie well before you saw her, and as soon as she entered a room she would certainly make her presence felt.

When Tony Visconti wrote to me sometime later after Angie had got a 9–5 office job, he even commented that 'at least the rest of the boys should be able to get some peace'.

On the other hand, there is no doubt that she was very devoted to David's success, and her actions and ideas were very important to his career. It was her idea to use costumes on stage. She definitely pushed him to experiment with different styles and images. He had obviously used stage make-up before from his time as a mime artist, but the idea of dressing up to be a different character in a rock band definitely came from Angie.

Nobody ever said this out loud, but it did seem to be very much a marriage of convenience, for both of them: she could work and live in London, while a green card meant David could work in America, which was obviously one of his great ambitions.

I'd never heard of such a thing as an open marriage before. I'd grown up in a stable, conventional family with a mother and father who were loving and faithful to each other, so there were a few shocks in store for me when I eventually moved in with them at Haddon Hall.

Once the recording sessions began, we soon learned that David had a very relaxed and quick way of working. He would only ever play the song through a couple of times, maybe three at the most, before we went in to record. We never had any rehearsals before the run-through either.

He would sit on a high stool facing us, holding his 12-string guitar. We'd record the backing track, with again only two or three takes at the most. David would record a guide vocal to help us with the timing and put the main vocal track on later.

He usually only ever did two or three takes.

Over the next few months, I recorded the following tracks at Trident Studios:

Unwashed and Somewhat Slightly Dazed
Cygnet Committee
Janine
Memory of a Free Festival   recorded after August, and again as a
                                 single in March 1970
Don't Sit Down   unlisted and mostly improvised 'yeah
                                 yeah'!
An Occasional Dream   I am credited with this but don't re-
                                 member doing it

God Knows I'm Good	I am credited but there is no percussion on this track
Letter to Hermione	again, I am credited but there is no percussion on this track

On Friday, 18 July 1969, Junior's Eyes had a break from David's album and recorded their own track 'Starchild' with a B-side, 'Sink or Swim', which was issued as a single in August 1969. This was also produced by Tony Visconti at Trident Studios, with Rick Wakeman joining us on mellotron.

'Grom' Kelly, the lead singer of Junior's Eyes, had a theory that 'Starchild' didn't do so well because it was confused with the track 'Good Morning Starshine', from the musical *Hair*, which was released at exactly the same time and was a big hit. I thought ours was a really good single and deserved more recognition than it got.

Rick's amazing playing had obviously caught the attention of producers like Tony Visconti and Gus Dudgeon – and this was still while he was at music college. He was later to hit the big time in the supergroup Yes, but was also a member of The Strawbs, and an incredible session musician, playing piano on 'Morning has Broken' by Cat Stevens and 'Life on Mars?' by David Bowie.

Before Mike Garson became Bowie's regular piano/keyboard player Rick was also invited to be a member of the original Spiders from Mars when David was assembling the Ziggy line-up a couple of years later. He turned David down in order to join Yes, who asked him on the very same day.

Tony Visconti produced the *Space Oddity* album. As I've mentioned, he was never a big fan of the 'Space Oddity' track, thinking it was a bit cheesy, so he gifted it to Gus, who thought it was wonderful. In my opinion he did a fantastic job. I didn't play on the single but I did play it live many times with David in Junior's Eyes and Hype.

A lot of books have Junior's Eyes listed as backing David at the famous Free Festival in Beckenham, held at the Croydon Road Recreation Ground in Beckenham, on Saturday, 16 August 1969. I can categorically state that Junior's Eyes were in Germany completing an eight-day run at the famous Star Club at the time, so it definitely couldn't have been us.

The festival, which inspired David's wonderful song 'Memory of a Free Festival', was a free gig to promote music in the community. (I played on both the single and album versions of this song.)

The September sessions included our recording of the album version of 'Memory of A Free Festival', which had been composed by David the previous month. By now I had got to know him really well and was used to his way of working. The procedure was exactly the same: David perched on his high stool with a 12-string guitar, poised to go through the numbers prior to recording them.

When the *Space Oddity* album was finally issued on the Philips label in late 1969, Junior's Eyes were given five copies each, and I couldn't wait to have a look at the gatefold sleeve to see my own name on a major recording. The album was actually called *David Bowie* (the name was changed to *Space Oddity* on rerelease).

Obviously, all of the songs were listed inside together with the lyrics to every song, but there was no mention of the musicians anywhere. I was gutted! The first album I'd ever played on, and with a recording star – and nobody would ever know I'd played on it. Tony Visconti said it was something to do with the record labels, David's being Philips and Junior's Eyes Regal Zonophone.

A few months later, when I had finally moved into Haddon Hall, I was in the room with David as he was looking at an album cover he'd just taken out of a large cardboard envelope. 'It's the American release,' he explained, 'and it's just been delivered to the office'. I didn't even know it was going to be released in America, so I was pleased to see it was very similar to the British version, only it was called *Man of Words/Man of Music* and was released on the Mercury label.

When I opened the cover, I was even more delighted to see that every musician who had played on the album had been credited, including me. There was my name: 'John Cambridge – drums'.

I said, 'Can I have that one, please, Dave?'

The main reason I wanted it was to show Angela, my mam and dad that I was finally making a success of my professional career now my name was officially linked to a rising star like David.

'But it's my only copy,' he protested.

'Oh go on, Dave, please.' I kept pestering him until eventually I wore him down and he gave me the album – complete with the packaging that it came in, which I still have.

I looked again at that album cover recently in preparation for writing this book and noticed something I've never picked up one before – indentations of what were obviously some doodles David had done on a piece of paper, using that album cover to rest on. I'm not sure what they are yet but they are definitely David's work; it looks like a couple of ETs or possibly a bird or an angel. A bit of forensic detective work is in order here, I think!

Once the *Space Oddity* album was released, David asked Junior's Eyes to accompany him on a series of promotional dates in Scotland in the autumn. I would now be working with him on a more regular, formal level – and live!

To get to the gigs in Scotland, we travelled up in David's newly acquired second-hand, grey Rover 100 and, of course, Junior's Eyes' trusty white Ford Transit van. As I mentioned earlier, Junior's Eyes, including Roger, all smoked. There was no way I was going to travel all the way to Scotland in a van filled with dope smoke, so I went in the car with David, driven by his friend Barrie Jackson.

We were going to be based at the same B&B in Edinburgh for the whole tour and would travel and return to the same digs after each nightly gig.

Our first Scottish gigs were:

Friday, 7 November was at The Blue Web, Salutation Hotel, Perth.
Saturday, 8 November The Grand Hall, Kilmarnock.

On the Saturday when we were due to leave the Edinburgh digs at lunchtime, I was still getting ready to go, finishing off in the bathroom. Edinburgh to Kilmarnock is 68.6 miles (I've Googled it!), so David and Barrie were going in the car as before and the rest of the lads in the van.

Everyone must have assumed that I was travelling in the other vehicle because the buggers left without me! Now, as I keep saying,- this is in the days before mobile phones, so I had no way of letting them know I was stuck and that they would arrive at the gig with no drummer! I had no option but to get the bus.

When I arrived at the bus station in Kilmarnock, I found by chance that it was right next door to the venue, because I happened to see Roger Fry, the roadie, unloading the equipment into the hall. How lucky was that? I could quite easily have been dropped off on the other side of town. Roger never batted an eyelid as I casually walked up; he just thought I'd got out of David's car. David, who thought I'd just got out of the van, didn't believe me until I showed them both the bus ticket.

And yes, of course I still have the bus ticket!

Saturday, 8 November Our second gig of the night, at the Community, Centre, Auchinleck, which is about ten miles south of Kilmarnock.
Sunday, 9 November The Kinema Ballroom in Dunfermline.
Monday, 10 November The final gig of this stint was at the Electric Garden in Glasgow, which had the reputation of being in a rough area of the city but also the place to play, like the Cavern in Liverpool or the Marquee in London.

We arrived at the gig early in the afternoon. As we entered, there was another band already set up and rehearsing. They turned out to be the support act and I'm sure they were called Verve (not Richard Ashcroft's). I remember closing my eyes and thinking as they played 'Suite: Judy Blue Eyes' by Crosby, Stills & Nash, how much they sounded like them. I often wonder what became of them (they probably think the same about us).

Edinburgh is a great place to stay, and David saw the sheet music for the 'Space Oddity' (a No. 5 hit by then) in a music shop window. Well, he just had to buy it, didn't he? (Wouldn't you?) I remember David coming out of the shop beaming, with a copy of it in his hands.

'They've got the bloody chords wrong!' he said, reading it as he was walking down the street.

On the same day in Edinburgh, we were in the Army & Navy Stores on Princes Street and David took a real liking to some three-inch wide, black leather belts with chrome buckles. 'How much?' he asked the assistant. 'A pound,' she replied. 'I'll take seven' he said and gave us all one each. Years later, my wife Angela threw that belt away, along with the polka dot tie that Ronno wore as Gangster Man in Hype, thinking it was 'tat'.

On 20 October, we recorded a Radio 1 show for Dave Lee Travis, but the next time we appeared live with Bowie was not until 20 November 1969, when we did the Purcell Room, a 'Showcase' gig at the Royal Festival Hall, London. It's funny but what I remember most about this gig is seeing David setting up a sort of merchandise/promo stall in the foyer, on his own, to promote the *David Bowie* album. He had all these album covers (no records inside) set up on the counter, like big greeting cards (it was a gatefold sleeve album).

The gig itself was great and he (and we) played really well – but apparently David was really pissed off because the music press had not been invited, as he'd been promised by Calvin Lee (a friend of Davis's) I remember the lonely sight of him collecting back all the empty album covers, again on his own, so Angela, my fiancée, went up to him and asked if he could spare one for her.

Without hesitation he gave her one and signed it:

> To Angie, Love and Peace and Best Wishes,
> David Bowie X

Autograph collectors will know that later on in his career, David never signed anything with 'David', just 'Bowie' and always put the year under the name, so this is a particularly unique piece of memorabilia – and one with unimpeachable provenance.

Junior's Eyes still had plenty of gigs on the books (without David) at this point, including another stint at the Star Club between 25 and 30 November just after the Purcell Room gig. I brought David a rubber Bowie knife back from Germany; he loved it and put it in his belt. I often wonder if he kept it, because he never threw anything away, apparently. The V&A 'David Bowie Is' exhibition was full of his old stage costumes and props.

We stayed in touch, as mates, after the recording of the *David Bowie/Space Oddity* album and obviously David was quite pleased to have a band at his disposal, so to speak – especially as he started to develop and write ambitious new material that he couldn't perform live as a solo performer. The rest of us were all earning a living from our gigs as Junior's Eyes and therefore not completely dependent on him for work, so our relationship was fairly relaxed.

When we played together, we travelled together just like any other band, and would always pitch in to help set up the gear and carry stuff in and out. I found out later that it all changed after Bowie hit the big time: he nearly always travelled separately to the Spiders and the Ziggy entourage.

When David played solo gigs, he would usually have just his 12-string guitar, but occasionally he used a maraca to accompany parts of his songs percussively. Even when we backed him at Junior's Eyes gigs, he nearly always had to have this maraca with him. It wouldn't fit into his guitar case, so was usually loose, and when we packed away the gear there was never anywhere to put it.

Once, I said: 'David, do you want me to pack this maraca away in my case, then you won't lose it?'

'Yeh, alright John, thanks,' he replied, which is how I came to have it. When I left Haddon Hall, I accidentally took it with me, and I still have it in my possession.

* * *

How many blokes could admit to sharing a bed with David Bowie?

I remember when we were living at St Helen's Gardens and were bored one night, Roger Fry, my roadie roommate, said: 'Let's go for a ride to Beckenham to see Bowie.' When we got there Angie (David's wife) was not around because she had gone to visit her parents in Cyprus. So it was just Bowie, Tony Visconti and his girlfriend Liz. I really liked Liz, but she would never tell me her surname. Just said, 'It's something to do with "jam".' I guessed 'Traffic? 'Robertson? Strawberry?' It was, in fact, 'Hartley.'

Tony and Liz usually kept themselves to themselves in their room, as they both had proper jobs to go to in the morning, but Roger and I stayed up chatting until quite late with Bowie, who suggested that rather than head back we stay the night. (Maybe he appreciated the company.)

'There's room for two,' David said, 'One in the bed, next to me, and one on the couch'.

Being a naïve and trusting young lad from the frozen north, I chose the bed, and had a very comfortable, good night's sleep, thank you.

All I can say is, it can't have put David off me because he asked us both if we'd like to move into Haddon Hall just after that.

We did a moonlight flit from St Helen's Gardens to Haddon Hall, 42 Southend Road, Beckenham, and when we eventually did move in, both Roger and myself slept on separate mattresses in what was David's living room, a communal area.

I've read that Mick Ronson, Trevor Bolder and Woody Woodmansey slept in the so-called 'creep' gallery when they stayed in the early days. Haddon Hall was certainly an old and atmospheric place and had a spooky kind of Gothic feel with a dark, sweeping staircase and big, stained glass windows. I personally never felt there was anything supernatural about it, even though Tony Visconti seems convinced there was a ghost there.

David confided in me that the telephone rang at 5.30 p.m. every day for a week just after his father died, on 5 August 1969. He said nobody ever answered when he said: 'Hello', and he was convinced that it was his dad, letting him know that everything was okay.

There were lots of laughs and pranks which lightened the atmosphere around the old place. Water pistol fights occasionally got quite competitive and I would sometimes have to feign surrender in a water fight, so I could then ambush David with a hidden Fairy Liquid bottle full of water.

A lot of this was just immature skylarking, kids playing practical jokes on each other, but it certainly gave us a lot of laughs and relieved the tension. David used to do this daft trick where he would pretend to thump you but stop his hand just short of making contact and at the same time hit himself. It made you flinch.

Tony Visconti bought a dartboard which we had in our room, where we would have tournaments. (David was only average at darts.)

There wasn't a lot of money around at the time for any of us and we barely got by on what we earned from music. For the most part we lived and ate simply and just enjoyed each other's company. Of course, whenever we got back late to Haddon Hall it was always tea and toast, more often than not with Marmite. I can't remember if David loved or hated it?

It was great to see the effect on him when fame began to get him noticed. I know David loved it when I put 'his record' on the jukebox upstairs in the 'newest pub in Beckenham' (local people will know the one I'm talking about) three times in succession. First and second times he just smiled, but then said 'What, again?' as it came on the third time. 'You bloody love it' I replied, which he did.

Over the next few years some of the greatest pop songs of the twentieth century were to be written at Haddon Hall and it became the launch pad for David's career. How sad that it has now been redeveloped, apparently into 42 flats. It could have been an English Graceland.

One of the great Bowie songs written at this time, and which was later rearranged and rerecorded for *Aladdin Sane*, was the track 'The Prettiest Star'. I remember watching David compose it, quietly strumming the chords and writing words which were to be quite prophetic about what was going to happen next in his life and career:

> *One day, though it might as well be some day*
> *You and I will rise up all the way, all because of what you are...*

He decided to record 'The Prettiest Star' as the follow-up single to 'Space Oddity'. I was asked to play on it, but it clashed with a Junior's Eyes gig. We did play it live many times in the gig set, and I ended up only recording the B-side, 'Conversation Piece', which was originally scheduled for *Space Oddity* but left off because there wasn't enough room.

We were walking home one day and David told me he was really pleased that the group Marmalade were going to do a cover of 'Janine', a song we regularly played live with him. For a songwriter it is always pleasing to hear that your material is appreciated in that way.

1969–70 was the threshold of the most important phase in David's career so far, and it was my privilege to both contribute to that and to get to know him better personally while living in the same house.

We talked and bantered like old mates now and there was a lot of trust between us. Sometimes it was just the little things that you take for granted with mates: David lent me the money to buy a glass-topped record deck from Germany when Junior's Eyes were playing at the Blow Up Club in Munich (without Mick Wayne) in January 1970.

There has been quite a bit of speculation over the years about David's older half-brother, Terry Burns, whom he mentions in several of his song lyrics, including famously in 'All The Young Dudes' ('My brother's back at home with his Beatles and his Stones'). I know David had been very close to him growing up and had been to see several big name rock and roll acts with him in the late 1960s. Terry had suffered serious mental health issues and spent time in Cane Hill Mental Institute, where he was being treated for schizophrenia.

One night after he'd been to visit David at Haddon Hall for the day, David, Roger and I took Terry to the bus stop in Beckenham in the van so he could get the bus back to Cane Hill. There were a few people waiting and Terry joined the end of the line as we waved him off. Then we went down the High Street to get a burger. When we looped round at the end to pass the bus stop again on the way back to Haddon Hall, the same queue was still there but Terry was gone.

'I know where he'll be,' said David, who was now concerned, and Roger pulled over.

Directly opposite the bus was a pub and David pulled open the door to find Terry leaning against the bar. 'I was just waiting for the bus,' he said, which had now gone. So we ended up taking him over 10 miles back to Cane Hill Hospital in Coulsdon. I remember being able to talk football with Terry in the back of the van, as he was very knowledgeable and could even name Hull City's forward line! (Not many current season pass-holders could do that.)

That wasn't to be my only encounter with David's family.

By the end of January 1970, Junior's Eyes was obviously running out of steam. Mick Wayne's partner, Charlotte, had been ill and he had missed a few gigs in the autumn, including all of the dates at the Blow Up Club in Munich. Tim Renwick now had other projects in the pipeline, so it was decided to wind the band up.

Our last gig together was to be on 3 February 1970 at the Marquee Club in London. This was the same gig where Bowie's new band Hype made their debut, with me on drums, Tony Visconti on bass and Tim Renwick (temporarily) on lead guitar.

In the audience that night, at my invitation, was my old Rats colleague and songwriter friend from Milford Grove on Greatfield Estate in East Hull, Mick Ronson.

* * *

Some of the less well-publicised details of that episode have become obvious to me only many years later. In researching this book and putting various pieces together, I've found out much more about what might really have happened.

So now's an opportunity for me to have my say, in writing.

Let's rewind slightly, to Tuesday, 6 January 1970, Junior's Eyes had just played the Charade Club in Rotherham when Tim Renwick asked if I could call Tony Visconti at the New Breed offices in Dumbarton House, Oxford Street. Tim was about to leave to join Terry Reid's band Fantasia, who were quite big in America, and since it now didn't look as if Mick Wayne would ever be returning, I was hopeful that it might be the offer of more London work – or, at least, something that might postpone an inevitable return to Hull.

So the next day, back in London, I went to speak to Tony in person in the office. 'Would you like to be the drummer in David's new band?' he asked. I was taken aback at first, but he happened to be in the middle of a call to David and passed the phone to me so I could speak directly to him.

'Why', I said, 'with the pick of all the drummers in London, would you want to choose me?'

'I like your drumming and I like you as a person,' David replied. 'I would like you to be in my new band'.

At that point, I was happy to accept.

The Speakeasy Club, at 48 Margaret Street just off Regent Street, was an upmarket central London venue, not far from Heddon Street, where David was later photographed for the cover of *Ziggy Stardust*, and a short walk through to Soho. Real Ziggy territory. Everybody had played there, from Jimi Hendrix to Cream, the Rolling Stones to Jeff Beck – in other words virtually anybody who was anybody on the music scene at the time.

On Thursday, 8 January 1970, David was booked to play there. It was his 23rd birthday and as the gig was originally meant to be a duo, just him and Tony Visconti, I'd gone along to watch.

'Are you in the van?' David asked, meaning *Have you got your drums with you*? I was, I did. 'Well, come on then, get set up!' he said. I suppose it was from that moment on that I was 'David's drummer'. There was a short Junior's Eyes tour in Germany, which we were obliged to complete, and the final farewell gig at The Marquee – and then I would be free of all other obligations.

This was also the night when I saw drumming legend Aynsley Dunbar sitting right at the front. Aynsley later played on David's *Pin Ups* album. He was a top session musician.

I opened the door for others to come down to London that September – and it wasn't long before I was paid a visit by The Rats lead vocalist, Benny Marshall. I suggested to David that Benny contribute some 'gob-iron' harmonica on David's 'Unwashed and Somewhat Slightly Dazed' track on the *Space Oddity* album. He did and is credited. He also accompanied playing Hype live playing at Hull University on 6 March 1970.

Back in Hull, word had obviously got around that I was now moving in more prestigious musical circles, playing big name venues and working in London with someone who'd enjoyed chart success.

By the time I was reunited with all The Rats, on Sunday, 28 September,1969 – at a free gig in East Park, Hull – a lot of water had gone under the bridge and we were all back on talking terms again with no hard feelings. After all, I seemed to be doing OK. It was almost as if they had done me a favour by causing me to leave and join the London scene!

So, when I overheard Bowie and Tony talking about looking to recruit a guitarist for David's new band the following February, I immediately thought of my old Rats bandmate Mick Ronson.

They were discussing their options, including various session musicians they had both worked with and people who were available at the time. Tim Renwick was, in fact, first choice – but as I said, he was about to go to work with Fantasia, who were making inroads in America, so he declined.

I offered to ask Ronno.

They probably thought, *A guitarist, from Hull? Pull the other one!*

I said, 'No, he's really good. Look, I'm going back home between gigs, let me bring him back with me, see what you think.'

I could just imagine what might be going through their heads. *What does he know about music, he's only a drummer. And anyway, what's he on about, a guitarist, from Hull? He's probably just one of John's old mates, some semi-pro with a daytime job. He's probably even a bloody gardener or something, pushing a wheelbarrow around all day.*

They casually waved me away.

But I kept pestering them, and in the end I asked them just to give him a listen. I'd bring him up to Haddon Hall for the new band's Marquee gig so they could see what he could do. Finally they both agreed, possibly more to pacify me; but they didn't show any real interest or enthusiasm.

In between gigs or recording I often used to go back to Hull, and the week after we came back from the Blow Up Club in Munich, I drove the Hillman Minx back up to see Angela and my family and to seek out Mick Ronson.

In his book *David Bowie: A Life*, Dylan Jones quotes Mick Ronson saying that he first got to meet David through Tony Visconti when he was recording *Fully Qualified Survivor* with Michael Chapman, that Trevor Bolder was in The Rats and that he was 'round at Dave's when he got the call from John Peel asking if he'd like to do the first Hype show with him' and so on. This just wasn't how it happened.

Mick had already been down to London in the summer of 1969 to play on Michael Chapman's album *Fully Qualified Survivor*, which had been produced by Gus Dudgeon – who, as we know, also produced David's single 'Space Oddity'.

There has been speculation about whether or not Visconti knew of Mick through Gus, but I'm certain Tony had never heard of him before – either by reputation, or even on the producer's grapevine. I say this confidently, remembering his and David's re-action to Mick's playing when he first plugged in his Gibson Les Paul a few days later.

When I went in search of Mick back in Hull, I found out from his mate Trevor at the depot that he was working for the City Council Parks Department and would be posted around different areas of the city with daily work details. This might mean landscaping, cutting grass, gardening and planting flowers or sometimes, like today, marking out sports pitches with creosote boundaries.

Eventually I managed to track him down to what is now Andrew Marvell College, right on the edge of East Hull.

This was Jarvis High School at the time and Mick's job that day was to refresh the lines on the school's rugby and football pitches. The school was very open and accessible, and anybody walking their dog or whatever could get on to the site.

I re-enacted this scene with Gary Kemp from Spandau Ballet, who was making a documentary about Mick in 2017, called *Passions*. Gary wanted to see for himself, and to film, where this 'historic' event had taken place. We had to go through all sorts of bureaucratic palaver with the school, and security is very strict, but the pitches are still there in exactly the same places.

As I pulled up, I could see Mick right in the distance. He was unmistakeable with his long blond hair, donkey jacket and wellies, and I shouted: 'Mick, Mick!'

At first, I thought he was pushing a lawnmower, cutting the grass, but he was definitely 'lining' with the creosote machine. As I got nearer, he stopped and looked a bit puzzled. 'Hiya, John. I thought you were in London with that Junior's Eyes band?'

I said, 'I am, but they're packing it in. Do you remember that kid David Bowie? He had a hit with his record 'Space Oddity'. You know, "Ground Control to Major Tom" and all that. Well, he's forming a new band and he needs a lead guitarist, so I said you might do it.'

'Oh no,' he said, adamant. 'I'm not going down there again.' And off he set again, with me following him! I think he'd got to the corner flag and turned right to do the touchline before I even caught him up. 'No, I've been ripped off so many times down there and I've got a proper job now. No thanks, I'm not interested.'

Well, I must have done three pitches with him, trying to persuade him (I never got paid, either!), but he kept insisting, he wasn't going to do it. I could quite easily have given up at this point and left, without any hard feelings or qualms, but for some reason I persisted. It seemed neither David and Tony in London nor Mick in Hull were interested in meeting, but I made a last desperate attempt. 'Look, we're playing the Marquee Club next Tuesday, and it's Junior's Eyes last gig. Why don't you just come along, bring your guitar and see what you think? It's the first gig for Bowie's new band

Hype too and Tim Renwick's standing in. I'll pick you up and you can come down with me if you like?'

I think his ears must have pricked up at the mention of the Marquee Club, which was another venue with a national reputation and one he knew well from his earlier stay in London. (And, of course, Jeff Beck had played there, many times.) It must have finally dawned on Mick that The Rats were only ever going to be a big fish in a little pond, locked into the north of England gig circuit and playing dance halls and clubs.

The opportunities that would come about by 'being seen' in London, especially after he'd just played on a record that 'would be sold in the shops' (Mick's words about *Fully Qualified Survivor*), plus guaranteed work with a name artist, was all a bit different from the scratching around that had happened with his last disastrous London experience.

Maybe, in his mind, this was also going to be his final shot at fame.

So he agreed, and on Tuesday, 3 February 1970, we loaded up and set off back to London in the Hillman Minx for me to play my last ever gig with Junior's Eyes. This was to be followed minutes later, by the first ever gig with my new band, David Bowie's Hype.

It was a very cynical, reluctant and shy Mick Ronson who came to watch this final gig at the Marquee Club in London that night, followed by (on the same bill and on the same stage) the debut of Hype – featuring me again on drums, Tony Visconti on bass, David on vocals and acoustic guitar and Tim Renwick temporarily on lead guitar (until a suitable replacement could be found).

We arrived at the Marquee around teatime just as Roger the roadie was setting up all the gear. Bowie hadn't arrived yet, so I said to Mick, 'You just sit down there and I'll be with you in a bit.' Junior's Eyes then played their last gig, and Bowie finally arrived for the debut Hype gig with Mick watching in the audience.

Afterwards I thought I'd better introduce them, so I said to David, 'Here's that kid I was telling you about, Mick Ronson.' David answered 'Oh, pleased to meet you.' Not much else passed between them until afterwards, back at Haddon Hall.

There were always acoustic guitars lying around at the Hall (see the photo) and Mick picked one up and started playing. David

David and John in a pre-match pose in the garden of Haddon Hall (photobombed by Nita Bowes, now Nita Clarke)

David, John and Angie Bowie (with a few 'neighbours') in the garden of Haddon Hall, Southend Road, Beckenham

David photographed by his manager, Ken Pitt, in a park close to Pitt's central London
apartment in Manchester Street

Mick Ronson arrives at Haddon Hall (John is having a haircut just left of shot)

David, Mick and John strumming guitars at Haddon Hall

David playing some of his songs to Mick and John at Haddon Hall

Bowie and The Hype gig at The White Bear pub in Hounslow

Bowie, Tony Visconti and John at The Hype's famous early glam rock performance at The Roundhouse. Taken by Ray Stevenson, March 1970

Two more Ray Stevenson Roundhouse photos, the bottom including Mick as 'Gangster Man', March 1970

Backstage at the Tin Machine gig in Bradford in 1989. David looking like he's getting ready to play cricket for Yorkshire!

Ched Cheesman, Tony Visconti, John Cambridge, Benny Marshall and John Bentley rehearsing for the Mick Ronson memorial gig at Hammersmith in 1994

Reunion between Mick Wayne and John

Front

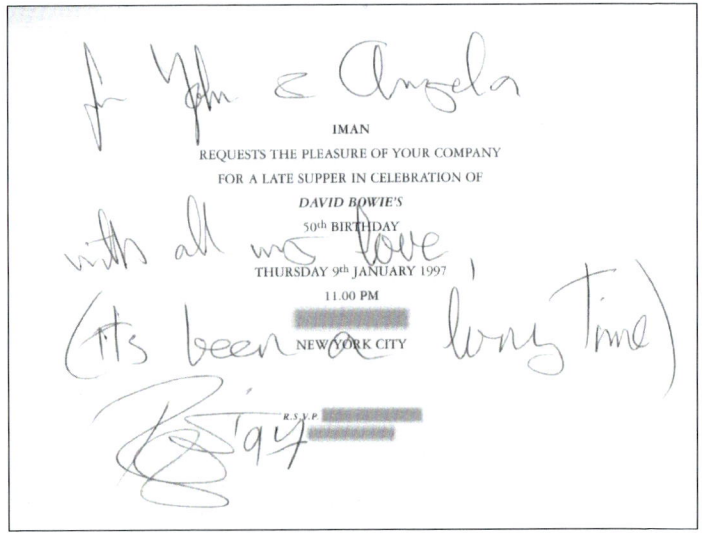

Back

The invitation to David's 50th birthday party in New York, complete with striking self-portrait illustration, January 1997

David and John reunite at the 50th birthday party

George Underwood and John at the 50th birthday party, David does some photobombing!

Joe Elliott and John at the after-show party following the Hull Ice Arena gig, 1997

Filming a sequence with Gary Kemp for the Sky Arts, Mick Ronson *Passions* documentary in 2016

Once again with David and George Underwood, this time backstage at Hammersmith, 2002

John, circa 2019, fending off blood-thirsty fans

joined in and they were just sort of jamming musical ideas together for about an hour. After a while the rest of us all went off to bed, but early next morning Mick and David, who at this point had obviously hit it off, just carried on from the night before, trading ideas and applying them to some of David's songs.

Then David made Mick the offer that would, I suppose, change the course of modern music.

'In a couple of days' time, I'm doing John Peel's Show. Would you like to do it with us?'

And that was it. Mick agreed. The first time Mick Ronson played a live gig with David Bowie and the first time he recorded with Bowie was at the Paris Cinema Studios in Regent Street, London for John Peel's *Top Gear* show on Thursday, 5 February 1970. (At the time of writing, this show and the next show are shortly to be released as an album entitled *The Width of a Circle*.)

I can't remember exactly how I felt at the time but I am sure that I must have felt some kind of vindication. Job done.

It was quite funny the way David introduced Mick on the show that night. It was as if he had some big secret present he hadn't been able to share with the world yet. He was undoubtedly impressed and was seemingly trying to encourage Mick to make a public commitment on air. He'd obviously already decided, as quickly as that, that he wanted Mick to be a long-term fixture.

Mick had only had a couple of days to learn David's material and suddenly, there he was, live with Tony Visconti and myself on national radio, playing songs from David's set, including:

Amsterdam (just David on 12-string acoustic and vocal)
God Knows I'm Good
Buzz the Fuzz
Karma Man
London Bye Ta-Ta
An Occasional Dream
The Width of a Circle
Janine
Wild Eyed Boy from Freecloud
Unwashed and Somewhat Slightly Dazed
Fill Your Heart (which was eventually recorded on *Hunky Dory*)

Waiting for the Man
The Prettiest Star (eventually resurfacing on *Aladdin Sane*)
Cygnet Committee

David played and sang really well despite the lack of rehearsal. Mick and the band sounded raw, with a couple of mistakes as you would expect, missed chords and slightly fluffed solos, but still good and definitely with a new energy brought by Mick.

Many of the tracks we recorded resurfaced later on *Bowie at the Beeb* and other rarity compilations – but as I said, it's the dialogue between Peel and Bowie which was really interesting and showed the impression David had already formed of Ronno.

'Are you going to be doing gigs with this band?' John Peel asks.

"Huh! Well, looking at them, no!' David replies at first. 'Yes. We're going to do some gigs, are we, Michael? Michael doesn't really know, he's just come down from Hull and I met him for the first time about two days ago through John the drummer, who's worked with me once.' (Cheeky bugger!)

'So you're planning to go on the road with them, as it were?'

'Yes, very surely.'

A lot of people said that they sensed a 'different energy' in the set that night, especially on the heavy tracks with rock power chords and long lead guitar solos. Tracks like 'The Width of a Circle' had a new strength that gave David good cause to be excited. He was obviously dazzled by 'Michael' (which was soon to change; only his family called him 'Michael', as far as I can remember). Likewise, Mick obviously saw in David what he had been forever seeking: a way to climb that elusive ladder to fame.

Here was somebody who could sing, write great original songs and who could perform confidently as a front man on stage with charisma and presence. In the documentary *Beside Bowie: The Mick Ronson Story* (2017), David says that he thought 'he'd found his Jeff Beck' – which would have been the highest compliment he could ever have paid to Mick, as we well know.

After the show and recording on the 5th, there were obviously a few practicalities to take care of if Mick was going to accept the offer to become a permanent member of Hype. Not least was that he had to go back to Hull, work his notice for his job at the council and then sort out things like the transporting of his amps, pedals, equipment and clothes, to move into Haddon Hall.

Fortunately there were no Hype gigs in the book until 22 February at the Roundhouse, London, and as David needed his grey Rover 100 servicing I suggested that, rather than pay extortionate London prices, he fill his car with petrol (which was a lot cheaper to do in those days) and travel north to see the sights of Hull and sort his car out there.

My old Rats' roadie mate, Peter 'Muff' Mirfin, had a 'proper job' as a mechanic by day, and said he would do the service for him for a fraction of the cost, at Turner & Sellers Auto Engineers in Hessle Square (which is still there).

David and Angie seemed quite happy to come up and meet our families, walk around and see the sights of Hull together – and sample some decent fish and chips at the Gainsborough Fish Restaurant in Hull Town Centre.

* * *

'Will they be needing the eiderdown?' my mam asked when she knew David and Angie would be staying with us. It was February and freezing when the Bowies eventually drove north to Hull. My dad used to be a real wind-up merchant and I was just praying he wouldn't do the 'pretending to sleepwalk' gag in his vest and underpants, which he'd inflicted on a couple of embarrassed visitors in the past. It would be interesting to see how they all got on with each other!

Mam and dad still lived in the same flat I'd grown up in Brisbane Street, when I'd shared a bedroom with my brother Ken. For all I knew, some of the drum kit might still have been on the shelf! Bowie was always a bookworm, so at least there would have been some bedtime reading if he'd wanted it.

David and Angie would be staying in Hull with my mam and dad while Tony Visconti and girlfriend Liz, who'd also decided to come up for a little break, would stay with the parents of my fiancée, Angela, eight miles north of Hull in Beverley. For those of you who have never been to Beverley, it is a beautiful town, like a little York. Tony and Liz pretty much spent their time doing the tourist thing and never really came out much with the rest of us, while my Angela went to work.

We would pick David and Angie up if we were going out and either walk around Hull city centre or, as we did one evening, go for a little drive into the countryside around Holderness and to a pub called the Railway at New Ellerby, near Hornsea. On the way back we also called in the Gardener's Arms pub on Cottingham Road near Hull University.

Both pubs are still there and going strong, even now. David really enjoyed drinking Cherry B and barley wine, which might sound an odd combination but had a very strong alcoholic content.

Somebody even said to him at the Gardeners' Arms that he 'looked like that singer David Bowie'.

'Do you know, a lot of people tell me that,' David replied, as we were going out through the door.

I often say to people in Hull who claim David Bowie did this and that, visited such and such a shop and went here and there, that to my knowledge there were only two places Bowie ever played in Hull: one was Hull University Student Union with Hype on 6 March 1970 and the other was The Phoenix Club (nothing to do with *Phoenix Nights*!). We went on Sunday dinnertime with Jim Simpson, my old Rats buddy, expecting to see some live music and ended up playing bingo. Which, by the way, we all thoroughly enjoyed.

The Bowies stayed in most nights to watch the telly and during the day ran up a huge phone bill on the house phone making unsuccessful trunk calls to northern universities to try to fix up further Hype gigs. They walked everywhere in Hull and I accompanied him to the *Hull Daily Mail* offices one afternoon for an interview, which was never used.

David got on really well with my dad – who, when I think about it, must have had an accent very similar to David's dad (they were born just over 10 miles apart); maybe he felt that connection too.

Dad complained afterwards that David had 'smoked all of his fags' too, but I don't think he would have minded really. David was very relaxed at our place and sat mostly on the floor with his back to the wall to watch the telly, just like another member of the family.

One morning, David got up and asked my dad, 'How are things today, Tom?'

The Phoenix Club, Hessle Road. The only other venue David Bowie played in Hull. During his stay in 1970 David played bingo with John, Jim Simpson (and Jim's dad), one Sunday lunchtime – just before the stripper!

My dad apparently replied 'Yes, hunky-dory, thank you.'

'Oh yes, and what does that mean?' said David.

I've read that other people have claimed David had also said the same to them too. But I do know that my dad told this story shortly after *Hunky Dory* came out, when he saw the album cover and remembered the conversation with David.

'He didn't even know what "hunky-dory" meant!' he said.

There has been a kind of urban mythology built up over the sources of some of David's lyrics, and people who claim they were the ones who he was writing about, or where he got a line for one of his songs.

It's common knowledge that the song 'Memory of A Free Festival' was inspired by the real free concert in Beckenham in August 1969, for example, and 'The Prettiest Star' was a love song apparently written for Angie (although some claim he had his former love Hermione Farthingale in mind). David drew on ideas and inspiration from people, events and encounters as well as books he'd read, films and artwork he'd seen.

It has also been claimed that Dad said: 'Look at those bloody cavemen go', about a gang of youths running down Brisbane Street beneath our flat window as David sat cross-legged on the floor. All I can say is that was the kind of thing my dad would say, so I wouldn't be at all surprised.

In his book *Starman: David Bowie*, Paul Trynka wrote that I was supposed to have seen David 'dancing with a bloke' at the Speakeasy Club just before he was due to marry Angie, and that when I warned him about what I thought would be Angie's reaction, he replied: 'John, I'm Only Dancing.'

Well, it's true that we had gone there one night for a drink and to see Toe Fat play (ex-Cliff Bennett and the Rebel Rousers) and yes, I did see David really 'going for it' and 'snogging' – but with a girl.

In fact, I never (ever) saw David 'dancing with a bloke' – that night or any other. And these were the days when if you were a 'vegetarian' it made the news! David's so-called open marriage to Angie seemed to be a green light for an unlimited number of intimate liaisons on both their parts. What's more, to be absolutely honest, I never saw evidence of male partners; there were many female 'visitors' to David and Angie's bedroom (lucky sod!).

I do remember one night David sheepishly opening the door of the bedroom when I was walking by, to some very loud shrieking and ecstatic moaning inside where 'dancing' was obviously taking place. 'I'll just leave them to it!' he said. 'Let them get on with it.'

So yes, it is possible that I am the 'John' of 'John, I'm only Dancing', just as it is very possible that my dad said things that gave rise to the line 'look at those cavemen go'. I would have loved to have been a fly on the wall to some of David and my dad's conversations; they would have been priceless. David always was a bit of an artistic magpie, and like lots of very creative people would take his inspiration from all sorts of different and sometimes unexpected sources.

* * *

I think David and Angela both really enjoyed the 'ordinariness' of staying with my mam and dad, and for David to be able to connect back with his Yorkshire roots, if only for a short while.

In the days, when more people wrote thank you letters than they seem to do now, Angie sent them a lovely note afterwards thanking them for their hospitality, which I also thought worth sharing here.

The letter was typed on the same typewriter on which David typed all of his song lyrics. It was addressed to 'Dearest Mum and

February 23rd. 1970

Flat 7,

42, Southend Rd.

Beckenham, Kent.

Dearest Mum and Dad Cambo,

Hello. Please forgive me for using the typewriter to write this letter to you, but Davie reminded me that it might be a good idea as my writing is so hard to read.... Also please let me ask forgiveness for taking so long in getting this note to you, but we found an enormous amount of work to be done when we returned from Hull and, believe it or not we have hardly stopped since. Your son is well and blooming although it is quite early in the morning as I'm writing the above, I saw him briefly in the kitchen organising Coffee and he seems in the best of health. God, I'm terrible you know, if I don't make a real effort, not to ramble on, I never actually get down to what I was going to say ; now before I go any further, let me thank you from Davie and myself for the most incredible time while we were in Hull, I hope that while we were there you could feel our appreciation instead of this letter being the thing to tell you, but I think you know why Im wanted to write and just let you know ' Officially' (don't laugh!) what marvellous Hospitality you possess. Anyway I won't write that any more because I have faith that you believe me and I want to tell you about other things. We did our first big gig at the Roundhouse last night and the boys went down very well, needless to say (my typing is getting as bad as my writing....) but we'll see if they are booked anywhere else as a result of last night and then we'll know how good a gig it really was,

All our Love, see you soon, be careful of that Weather in Hull and the sense of Humour, I understand it's catching..........

Angela   L. David

Angie Bowie's letter to Mam and Dad, February 1970

Dad Cambo' ('Cambo' was always my nickname, and still is), and dated 23 February 1970.

> Flat 7
> Haddon Hall
> 42 Southend Rd.
> Beckenham, Kent

'Dearest Mum and Dad Cambo,

Hello. Please forgive me for using the typewriter to write this letter to you, but Davie reminded me that it might be a good idea as my writing is hard to read… Also please let me ask forgiveness for taking so long in getting this note to you, but we found an enormous amount of work to do when we returned from Hull and, believe it or not, we have hardly stopped since. Your son is well and blooming although it is quite early in the morning as I'm writing the above, I saw him briefly in the kitchen, organising coffee, and he seems in the best of health. God, I'm terrible you know, if I don't make a real effort, not to ramble on, I never actually get round to what I was going to say; now before I go further, let me thank you from Davie and myself for the most incredible time when we were in Hull, I hope that while we were there you could feel our appreciation instead of this letter being the thing to tell you, but I think you know I wanted to write and just let you know 'Officially' (don't laugh!) what marvellous hospitality you possess. Anyway I won't write that anymore because I have faith that you believe me and I want to tell you about other things. We did our first big gig at The Roundhouse last night and the boys went down very well, needless to say (my typing is getting as bad as my writing…) but we'll see if they are booked anywhere else as a result of last night and then we'll know how good a gig it really was.

All our love, see you soon, be careful of the Weather in Hull and the sense of Humour, I understand it's catching……

Angela & David xx'

* * *

I often wonder what people would have been prepared to pay for a private gig by David, especially after he really became famous. When I think of all the times he played to only a handful of people in the Arts Lab in Beckenham, or in pubs where there was barely enough people to be called an audience – and if there was, they were often uninterested or noisy – well, what would those same people have stumped up to see him in the '80s in an arena gig or at Live Aid? I was privileged to see him strumming his guitar every day. There was always a guitar, usually his 12-string, lying around and anyone could pick it up and noodle around.

I remember how David once taught me to play 'Space Oddity' on the guitar. He just showed me where to move my fingers and how to make the chord shapes for the accompaniment, as I didn't know the names and shapes of any chords at the time.

I also listened to him compose 'The Prettiest Star', which he said he had written for Angie.

Another time I remember sitting down next to David as he was playing one of his new songs. Angie was sitting next to him on the other side as he began strumming and she joined in, in a very high-pitched voice, singing the chorus which included the words 'Oh by Jingo'. I said, 'Yes, Dave, that sounds alright that'. David just looked at me and glanced at Angie as if to say, 'John, don't encourage her.'

I didn't realise for years after that this would become the song 'After All' on *The Man Who Sold the World* album, which was recorded two or three weeks after I left Hype.

Angie idolised David and eventually she did go out and get a job while David just spent all day, every day playing and composing music. He was always trying out ideas and seemed to have a lot of material 'in his head' already composed. A lot of his lyrics were just hand-written scribbles at first, which he would then shape up on his little typewriter. He would just sit there singing different lines and trying out chords to go with them – a bit like Paul McCartney's singing 'Scrambled Eggs' as he wrote 'Yesterday' – trying to get the right rhythm and tone. If only we'd had mobile phone cameras then to record it. A lot has been written about David's creativity and especially the way he played with lyrics and sounds, and it would have been fascinating to capture his imaginative methods in process.

In March 1970, just after Mick had joined me in Hype, I was at his house on Greatfield Estate with his girlfriend Denise and my fiancée Angela, when his mum Minnie offered to make us a cup of tea or coffee.

Being a big tea drinker, I naturally said, 'Yes, please'.

I don't think there was such a thing as teabags in those days, so the hot water was poured onto the loose leaves in your cup, which sometimes left a load of bitty black dregs at the bottom when you'd finished.

When I'd finished mine. Minnie offered to read the tea leaves, which was something she did on a regular basis, apparently. (This might also have explained Mick's interest in the palm-reading Romanies from Yarmouth.)

'Someone in this group is going to cause a lot of trouble,' she said, when she had finished. Because I was always the joker in the pack, both Angela and I got the impression that she must have meant me.

I'm not usually a superstitious type (touch wood), but there were three other people in the room that night (four including Mick's mum) – and I've often wondered, given what happened shortly after, if that was actually the case.

The new band, now complete with Mick on guitar, were called Hype. According to Ken Pitt, the name came about when he was talking to David about 'hyping up' maximum publicity for the band. David said, 'The whole thing is one big hype'. So Ken suggested 'Why not just call the band *Hype*?' and David agreed. Funnily enough, I've recently found out that photographer Ray Stevenson, a good friend of David's, has also said that he suggested the name.

The band was relatively short-lived in terms of gigs and recordings (I've listed all the Hype gigs I played in Appendix 4). David, 'the boys' and I would come back to Hull to play Hull University Student Union on 6 March (a gig he had fixed up from my mam and dad's phone) and then we had a rebooking at the Roundhouse for The Atomic Sunrise Festival five days later.

As Angie Bowie said in the letter to my mam and dad, we had already done the first one at the Roundhouse, and we were now looking for more publicity and profile to market the new group and get us known. One night the conversation turned to what we actually wore on stage, and Angie and Liz began to discuss our stage costumes. Never mind the usual denims and T-shirts (or corduroys and jumpers) hey decided we needed more striking stage outfits.

As a result, Hype are often credited with playing the first ever Glam Rock gig at The Roundhouse on 11 March 1970. This was the outset of a decade which would soon be dominated by Bowie's music both in the UK and abroad, and some writers believe it was fitting that he should kick-start the decade with something controversial and 'different'.

There is some poor-quality grainy footage on YouTube of that gig, owned by Adrian Everett, who in 1990 rescued 33 hours of 8mm film footage of the entire 'Atomic Sunrise' festival, which was rotting in canisters. We are playing Lou Reed's 'Waiting for The Man', but as there was no sound on the original film footage, another live recording of us playing that same track has been dubbed over the top. There were various photos taken at the gig too.

On the same bill that night we followed a young, up-and-coming band called Genesis, led by Peter Gabriel, who also had a taste for wearing striking and bizarre costumes in the early days.

David was dressed as the so-called Rainbow Man, wearing a silver jacket, a chain type belt, sparkly silver lurex tights and a pair of buccaneer-style, thigh-length boots. Mick Ronson was in a gold Gangster Man outfit with polka dot tie, a suit that actually belonged to David, and Tony Visconti on bass wasn't quite Superman in a cape and skin-tight suit with H for Hypeman on his chest. Unfortunately, with his dark goatee beard, Tony ended up looking more like Ming the Merciless from *Flash Gordon* than anything.

What I was called?

Yes, that's me: Cowboyman. The Cambo Kid rides again.

Cambo the Cowboyman with a few frills sewn onto my shirt, a white ten-gallon cowboy hat and a waistcoat (which I can still get into). I did buy a cowboy scarf, but that doesn't fit me now. Too tight.

In the front row was David's old friend Marc Bolan, watching our every move. He was wearing a child's plastic Roman soldier breastplate bought from Woolworths', and was photographed resting on his arms. But at least he was trying to join in and entering into the spirit.

I'm going to take another opportunity to set the record straight: Dylan Jones claims I was dressed as a pirate!

A pirate? Come off it, Dylan.

He should have checked with me.

Tony Visconti says, in his book *Bowie, Bolan and the Brooklyn Boy*, that we were heckled by a few wags in the crowd that night, with homophobic insults such as 'faggot' and 'poof' levelled at us. According to him, 'all of our clothes' were stolen from the dressing room after the gig, so we had to travel home through the cold March London night, like Del Boy and Rodney, still in our superhero costumes.

I must have been pretty shielded at the back because I don't remember it being like that from my perch on the drum stool. Maybe it was Ronno's loud guitar which drowned out all audience noise for me because I didn't hear any of it. As for the clothes being stolen, I arrived in the outfit I would be wearing on stage, so it made little difference to me. (I didn't have a very extensive wardrobe in those days anyway.)

But, I do still have the cowboy hat, the waistcoat I wore that night – and I use the hat as a prop as I tell this story in *Turn and Face the Strange*, the show about Mick Ronson. What's more, it's the same drum kit I play.

We did don those costumes again for just one more Hype gig and got a mixed reception. At the Sunderland Locarno Ballroom on 13 March, the northern audience was equally lukewarm about the stage costumes, so that was the end, for now, of dressing up.

Reviews for the new Hype line-up were mixed, despite Angie's attempt to paint a positive picture to my mum and dad. *Disc and Music Echo*, 14 March 1970, said:

> *This show was a disaster. He needs an expert on sound balance who should effectively solve the teething problems of the new line-up.... The volume on Mick Ronson's lead guitar was so high that not only did he block out David's singing, but he also completely overpowered John Cambridge's drums. The volume also cleared the seats in a direct line with his speaker.*

THE happy STAR HOTEL ✶ W. CROYDON

296 London Road, Broad Green

Monday, March 30th
LIGHTS **DAVID BOWIES HYPE**

SOUNDS ➕ UGLY ROOM

We are changing our night to Fridays and are pleased to begin with
BLACK SABBATH on FRIDAY, APRIL 3rd

Star Hotel advert; John's last gig with Bowie

I did read that in an effort to prevent Mick being overwhelmingly loud on one of the Ziggy tours the road crew altered the knobs on his amplifier, Spinal Tap style, so they only turned up to 8. There was one final gig with this line-up and that was at the Star Hotel in Croydon, close to David's home in Kent. I can't remember too much about this particular evening except that it was a usual sort of pub gig and not that busy. As it turned out though, it was the last time I performed live with David.

My friend John 'Hutch' Hutchinson also lived and worked with Bowie in the band Feathers. In his excellent book *Bowie and Hutch*, he says that I was Bowie's best man. I suppose I'll go along with that, seeing as I am one of only two people who can claim that honour – his son, Duncan, is the other, performing the role at David's marriage to Iman twenty-two years later. When somebody once asked if I'd been at his wedding, even David answered straightaway: 'But you were my best man, weren't you, John?'

It could hardly be said I performed a traditional best man's duties at David's civil ceremony wedding to Angela Barnett on 20 March 1970 at Bromley Register Office, though. There were no speeches, no fumbling about in pockets for rings, no thanking the bridesmaids. I attended because I'd been invited the night before, along with Clare Shenstone, to be one of the witnesses. Clare was a folk singer, artist and actress and spent the night before the wedding with David and Angie at Haddon Hall.

When the registrar called for witnesses to step forward, Margaret 'Peggy' Jones (David's mum) jumped forward and took my place! I remember David turning round to me and sort of shrugging his shoulders as if to say, *Sorry, mate, I couldn't help it.*

BOWIE CONCERT

DAVID BOWIE, whose new single "Prettiest Star" is just released, stars in a solo concert at London's Royal Albert Hall tonight (Thursday). He also plays solo dates at University of Surrey, Stag Hill, Guildford (Saturday), and Three Tuns, High Street, Beckenham (19).

David will be backed by his newly-formed group, Hype, at a date at Fillmore North, Locarno, Sunderland next Sunday (14). The group comprises David's producer, Tony Visconti (bass), John Cambridge (of Juniors Eyes) on drums, and Mick Ronson (guitar).

Melody Maker, 14 March, 1970

Bowie's bow

DAVID BOWIE, in ten-league boots and groovy gear, presented his new backing group line up Hype, at London's Regent Street Polytechnic on Saturday. He needs an expert on sound balance who should effectively solve the teething problems of the new line up.

David had much more confidence and stage presence with this backing group, and as his songs are suitable for grooving to as well as just listening to, the brightest hope could well change categories.

This show was a disaster. The volume on Mick Ronson's lead guitar was so high that not only did he block out David's singing but also completely overpowered John Cambridge's drums. The volume also cleared the seats in a direct line with his speaker.

That magic that makes for greatness is there but suppressed, sometimes even hidden. If my ears ever recover I expect to see David plus Hype in a few months time . . . shining through.

GAVIN PETRIE

Disc and Music Echo, 14 March, 1970

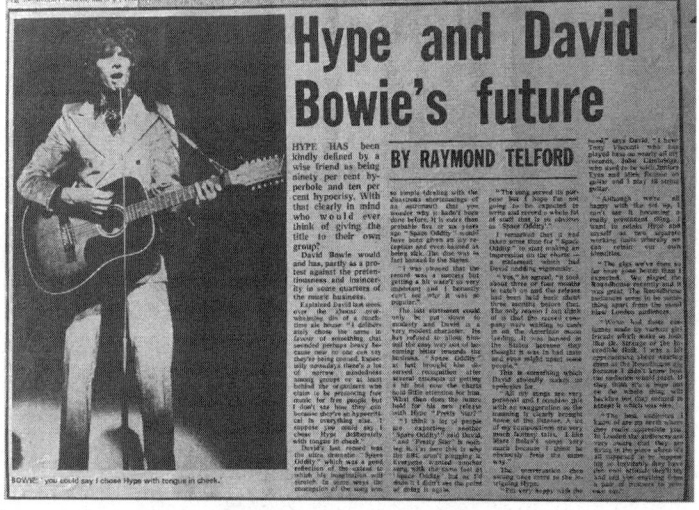

Hype and David Bowie's future

BY RAYMOND TELFORD

Bowie and Hype articles from John's scrap book, March 1970

NEW MUSICAL EXPRESS

Friday, week ending March 21, 1970

BACKING GROUP FOR BOWIE

David Bowie has formed his own backing group to accompany him on personal appearances. Known as The Hype, it includes record producer Tony Visconti on bass, as well as John Cambridge (drums).

I'd never seen Peggy at Haddon Hall before and she hadn't actually been invited to the wedding. Apparently, she'd seen the announcement in the local press and turned up in a nice twin set and matching hat anyway.

I felt really honoured that of all the people around he'd asked me. (Although I do now know that Tony Visconti was working that day.)

Then came the now famous photos, taken by the local press (tipped off by Peggy) outside Bromley Registry Office, which featured David in his furry, hippy Afghan coat and scarf, Angie in a flower-patterned hippy dress and Peggy in the middle.

Chapter 4
THE SACKING

This could have been the most difficult part of the story for me to write, but it is probably also the part I have wanted to write most – not least to just sort in my mind what actually happened that led to the derailing of my career as a professional musician. On reflection, what occurred was a clumsy and unpleasant business that might have threatened friendships with people I had grown really close to, and whom I'd gone out of my way to help.

On Wikipedia there is an explanation of why I left Hype, which is nothing more than fake news. It's interesting to see what they had to say. Surprise, surprise: like a lot of versions, much of it is just wrong.

In April 2021, here's what it said:

The band Bowie assembled comprised John Cambridge, a drummer Bowie met at the Arts Lab [not true!], Tony Visconti on bass and Mick Ronson on electric guitar. Known as Hype, the bandmates created characters for themselves and wore elaborate costumes that prefigured the glam style of the Spiders from Mars. After a disastrous opening gig at the London Roundhouse, they reverted to a configuration presenting Bowie as a solo artist. Their initial studio work was marred by a heated disagreement between Bowie and Cambridge over the latter's drumming style [definitely not true]. Matters came to a head when an enraged Bowie accused the drummer of the disturbance, exclaiming 'You're fucking up my album' [utter bollocks]. Cambridge left and was replaced by Mick Woodmansey.

First of all, I never decided 'to leave and go back to Hull', as Karen 'Gilly' Larney writes in *Mick Ronson: The Spider with the Platinum Hair*. It was never my decision, although that's what happened on the morning of 7 April 1970: I left and returned to Hull, as I simply wasn't required anymore in the band. Although I stayed in touch with David for the rest of his life, and remained really good friends, we never discussed my leaving or what was behind it.

Fifty years on, I'm not so naïve to think this sort of thing doesn't happen in all walks of life, especially in bands – or anywhere that personnel changes are made, in industry, business or schools. People will always be promoted or move on, as young talent comes through, when deals are done and promises made behind people's backs. Career casualties are inevitable.

In the latter years of David's career, he used a fairly stable group of musicians, more or less as a backing band, featuring artists such as the brilliant bassist Gail Ann Dorsey and pianist Mike Garson, but at the point I left he was still experimenting with identities and images. He was always incredibly ambitious and driven to succeed. He needed the all-important breakthrough soon in order to get wider recognition and reward for his talents – and he could see straight-away how Ronno was going to help accelerate that breakthrough.

David's collaborators were chosen to suit the phase, concept or type of sound he wanted. He worked with jazz musicians, with Brian Eno, and with the rock band Tin Machine and duetted with many others, including John Lennon, Mick Jagger, Queen, Arcade Fire, Dave Gilmour, Cher, and Robert Fripp – the list goes on.

In a post-show Q&A for *Turn and Face the Strange* at Hull Truck Theatre, I was asked why I left Bowie, so I will try to answer that question now.

On 24 March 1970, Tony Visconti booked me to play on Marc Bolan's single 'Oh Baby', which was to be recorded under the pseudonym of Dib Cochran & the Earwigs (a funny name and insect – would this be echoed latter Ziggy Stardust and the Spiders?). The other artists appearing on the record were Tony himself on vocals and bass, Marc Bolan on guitar and vocals and, once again, Rick Wakeman on keyboards.

This single never did anything in the charts, and both 'Oh Baby' and its B-side 'Universal Love' slipped into obscurity not very long after its release. Nowadays it is apparently very collectable and just a few years ago a sample-stickered copy sold for £609.99 on eBay.

Meanwhile Mick and David had thrown themselves into writing and practising and would frequently shut themselves away for hours to rehearse and try out new ideas.

I would occasionally put my head round the door, only to be told things like 'Hang on a minute John, we just need to do this.' (In other words, 'Piss off!') I didn't mind this so much, but when it came to having to learn something new or complicated to record, it didn't give me enough warning and rehearsal time to get it right, especially the way David and Mick wrote and arranged things so quickly together.

In April 1970 David clearly sensed that his stars were finally beginning to align, and Mick Ronson was clearly going to play a crucial role.

'The Prettiest Star' had bombed, selling less than a thousand copies, and he now desperately needed to get back the momentum and the success of 'Space Oddity' – or become just another one-hit wonder.

As for Mick, he clearly saw in David something that had always been missing from The Rats. That same something which Mick and I had tried to address with our little attempt at writing 'Bernie Gripplestone'. David was a songwriter, a creator who could write stunningly original material – and had won an Ivor Novello award, for 'Space Oddity', to prove it.

Mick on the other hand, was an amazingly inventive arranger, producer, interpreter and 'improver' of songs, especially the kind of songs that David wanted to develop David was now moving away from the 'hippy folk' material dominated by 12-string acoustic guitar, to a heavier rock and roll sound and Mick would play a key role in this transformation. He certainly had the musicianship, stagecraft, experience and good looks to stand on equal terms as an artist and performer.

This also meant that David could relax much more as a writer and frontman, knowing that Mick would take care of the band and the arrangements. It was a perfect professional marriage.

In my 1970 diary I've written: Monday 23 February (Trident Studios) David Bowie (11–4) 'Memory of a Free Festival'. We were booked in for 11–4 at night! (not many musicians are up before 11 in the morning!). The session was initially to do 'Memory of a Free Festival (Parts 1 & 2)'. I had already played both tracks on David's album, but this was going to be for a single version with a drum track running right through.

Tony had also arranged some new parts for a Moog synthesiser. In 1970, this was a relatively new instrument; it debuted in 1964. Tony, David and myself had gone to see one just a couple of days earlier – there were only two in the country at the time and we had to hire it for the session.

The first part of the recording went well and we got through the backing track quite quickly. It was quite easy for me because I had played the song regularly with David, and the single arrangement was quite similar to the original. Tony said he really liked the intro especially because we all came in at different times.

Now it came to the overdubbing of the Moog track.

Mick had already shown he could play piano (he was a really gifted pianist), so he would be the one to put on the Moog track, assuming that it was like a piano or organ keyboard to play. It was Mick's first time in Trident with David and Tony, and he obviously wanted to make a good impression, so he went downstairs into the studio for a run-through while we all stayed upstairs in the console looking down at him.

Now I'm no Rick Wakeman, but the Moog turned out be a real twat to play. It seemed to go out of tune as one note cancelled out another, and Mick kept cocking it up. By sheer coincidence, there was a very smartly dressed guy in the studio working in another part of the building, who kept popping in to see Tony. It turned out to be Ralph Mace, an experienced musician who knew what he was talking about and who seemed to be able to help.

First of all, he pointed out that the Moog was not in tune with what we were recording. He asked if Tony could play him some of the track, which he did. Mick, who was with Ralph at this point, then played just one note to check whether the Moog was in tune and Tony actually left that one 'rogue' note on the final single re-cording. Just listen to it; it's just as David comes in with the word 'that': 'Oh to capture just one drop of all the ecstasy that swept that afternoon'.

Ralph then went on to play through the whole rest of the song effortlessly. Tony and David thanked him for playing a session he wasn't even booked for, and for saving them wasting money on the hire of the Moog. (I bet Ralph has told this story a few times over the years!)

The end of the song changes tempo before moving into Part 2: 'The sun machine is coming down and we're gonna have a party', and Tony was wondering how to merge the two parts smoothly.

So I made a suggestion to him about the arrangement: 'Why don't I hit a cymbal with my felt bass drum beater to give a gong effect, then play it backwards so that it seems like the sound sucks in to a dead stop? Then start Part 2.'

We had already tried something like this with Mick's guitar solo on 'The Rise and Fall of Bernie Gripplestone' by The Rats, a few years earlier at Keith Herd's studio in Willerby when we were playing with reversing sound as the Beatles did with 'Taxman'. This was very much a '60s thing, inspired by Paul McCartney and George Martin's work on psychedelic tracks like 'Tomorrow Never Knows'. Tony liked the idea and built it into the arrangement. So that's what you actually hear on the final recording.

Once we got onto Part 2, it was a lot easier. A crowd of us (not including David) stood around the mic to sing the big crescendo of the chorus 'The sun machine', just like in 'Hey Jude'.

Marc Bolan was also a member of the chorus and we sang virtually the same arrangement as the album. Marc had a red and black jumper on and with his hair looked like Dennis the Menace. As we were singing, Marc and I did a synchronised dance routine during the 'sun machine is coming down', flinging our arms up and stepping in time just like The Four Tops or The Temptations.

Tony Visconti's voice came booming over the monitor: 'Be careful with him, John, he's worth a million!'

Not long afterwards he was – and more!

Listening to the Part 2 playback, Mick suggested to David, 'Why don't you put some Paul Rogers style, ad lib "Yeah, Yeah, Yeahs" over the chorus?' And David, who was really good at pushing people forward and letting them express themselves, just looked at Mick and very dryly said, 'You do it.' Mick thought he was joking at first but was eventually persuaded – and that was his first studio recording with Bowie.

So all of the 'Yeah, Yeah, Yeahs' at the end of 'Memory of A Free Festival, Part 2' (single version) are, in fact, Mick Ronson.

Not a lot of people know that.

In some books and even on the *Space Oddity* CD issued by Rykodisc, Woody is credited playing on 'Memory of A Free Festival'. I thought that they must have rerecorded the drum part. When I listen to the single, though, my thoughts are that unless Woody has copied my drumming beat for beat it sounds just like me.

This was cleared up when we did the Mick Ronson Memorial Concert at The Ice Arena in Hull in 1997. I was sitting backstage at the bar with Woody and Kevin Cann and I asked Woody if he had ever rerecorded 'Memory'. Woody said, 'No, I don't think we even played it live.' So there you go, Kevin (a friend and an authority on all things related to Bowie), I knew it was me (case dismissed).

At the recording session, we got through 'Memory' quite quickly, and still had some studio time to spare, so it was suggested that we have a go at 'The Supermen', another new song written by David at Haddon Hall.

We had performed this song live at the 'dressing-up gig' at the Roundhouse but can't have done it together more than a couple of times. During the afternoons before the recording David and Mick ('Piss off, John') had been going through some new stuff on guitars, suggested by Mick. This new arrangement included a new bit involving a more complex drum fill. Sometimes I wish I'd been allowed in on that afternoon when they had locked themselves away, I could at least have had some idea of what to expect of the new part. After all I knew the song well enough to play it live. The new tricky bit had a stop, start accent, which I had to do with drum fills in between. And I kept getting it wrong.

After a few takes, Mick came right up to the drum booth window and quite aggressively shouted in my face: 'Come on, it's fucking easy.' Well, that didn't help at all. If anything, that made it worse; the pressure was really on me now. At this point David, who could see how I felt, intervened and said, 'Come on, John, let's have a break and go for a drink.' We went together with Angie to the La Chasse Club, not far away in Wardour Street while Mick and Tony stayed at the studio.

La Chasse was a little Soho club up some stairs, where musicians used to go to chill and drink after gigging or recording. You could bump into anybody in there. It was always full of artists and musicians.

I know this might sound like just a silly little anecdote, but it is one that will always stick with me. It was probably funnier at the time, and we needed a lift after the tension of the last recording session and Mick's 'bad Moog'.

Somebody in the club had one of those joke-shop laughing bags, a battery-operated contraption that plays a really daft, exaggerated 'laughing policeman' chortle. Its owner must have had a drink or two, but he was also getting increasingly mad at this contraption which he now couldn't turn off.

David knew him and said he was one of the band Ashton, Gardner and Dyke (who went on to have chart success with 'Resurrection Shuffle'). In the end, out of sheer frustration, the man threw this contraption at the wall. Instead of it smashing to pieces, though, it hit the floor and continued to laugh.

David, Angie and I fell about laughing, which really lifted the mood and cheered me up. When we went back to Trident, now relaxed, we had another go at 'The Supermen' part and I got through it in the first take.

I often wonder what the conversation was between Mick and Tony when we were out – and whether it was at that point they discussed replacing me with Woody Woodmansey. Perhaps my not being able to play the new part straightaway was the excuse they needed to suggest getting somebody new.

It took a few years before I could bring myself to listen to the album recording of 'The Supermen' on *The Man Who Sold the World* with Woody Woodmansey drumming. When I did, lo and behold the 'tricky bit' I'd found so hard wasn't even in. There were none of the difficult stops and starts Mick had got so angry about me not getting right first time!

By sheer coincidence, as I'm writing this, Marc Riley, formerly of The Fall and now Radio 6 DJ, rang to ask me if it is me playing on a demo version of 'The Supermen' which is due to be sold at auction in Warrington. I listened to it and it is a version I did (minus 'tricky bit' again) – but which I didn't even know existed.

I have to use this opportunity to say definitively now that at no point did David ever say: 'You're fucking up my album', as Christopher Sandford writes in *Bowie: Loving the Alien*. He writes too that I was a 'victim of David's ego', another assumption I really resent and have never felt was the case.

David never used language like that to me – there was never a cross word between us. If anything, it was Mick who lost his temper that day and swore.

Sandford contacted me asking for help with his book and actually lists me as a collaborator in his acknowledgements, even though I declined the offer to help him with the section. He even sent me two letters asking for interviews, but the only time I ever spoke to him was when he followed up the letters with a phone call. As you can see, 'You're fucking up my album' has now crept into Wikipedia too.

I know that when a new football manager takes over a club he often wants to bring in his own staff – coaches and physios and the like – to have a fresh start and to be in complete control. Mick had been given the green light to do whatever he needed to get the new band ready.

I had been recruited to Hype by David less than two months earlier when he said he 'liked my drumming and liked me as a person'. Tony Visconti said he liked my 'no frills drumming' and that I 'lifted everybody'. And from my later contact with David I know that the light-heartedness and humour was something he really valued, well before all the craziness of fame, drugs and complicated relationships. We had a bloody good laugh together, in a relationship that continued right up until his death.

But now, at this point, it seemed my face didn't fit – and I wouldn't be the only casualty.

I found I was going to be replaced, more or less a year to the day since I had been sacked from The Rats.

On 6 April 1970, I was balancing on the stepladder at Haddon Hall, painting the ceiling, when David and Angie pulled up in the car on the gravel drive outside. The sash window was open and I could hear the car doors close. Something was up.

'David, you've got to tell him,' I heard Angie say.

'But he's a mate,' said David. My heart sank. They were talking about me.

David asked me to come off the stepladder and to sit down, he had something to tell me.

'I'm sorry, John,' he said. 'We've been talking and we've decided that we're going to get another drummer. I want you to know it's not you, John, it's just we need someone who is going to help with the arrangements. It's really important. You don't have to leave, you can stay here with us for as long as you like. This isn't about you, John.'

I said I would go straightaway but David repeated that I didn't have to.

I didn't have much money, so I asked if he could lend me £5 so I could get home.

And that was it.

In his book, Tony Visconti said he was 'surprised' that Mick had 'instigated' my sacking in order to bring in Woody Woodmansey. But the backdated contract with Philips records had been signed by them days before David told me. A mere seven weeks before, Tony

The Haddon Hall stepladders on which John was sacked!

had been the one to broker the job of drummer to me in David's new band. Yet Tony had supposedly said 'we were thinking of replacing John anyway.' So what had changed?

In his book, Woody says that he and Mick 'had an understanding that they'd play together again', even as Mick set off to live in Haddon Hall in February 1970. Mick had actually said to Woody after breaking up The Rats 'I'm sorry, Woods, I really am. But don't worry, we'll sort something out.' He seemingly had plans to reunite with him as soon as possible.

Perhaps Woody and I should both have seen we would both eventually become disposable, and casualties of other people's ambitions.

David was the one who had made fame possible for everyone else. He was the creative one, the breadwinner, and I know he didn't want anybody to compromise centre stage or delay him making the breakthrough he so desperately sought.

But Mick was equally driven and it appears he was quite prepared to sacrifice others in order to fulfil his own dreams. There was also that awkward time when we'd rehearsed secretly with Robert Palmer behind the back of our Rats lead singer Benny Marshall which showed me early on how driven Mick could be.

In his book *Any Day Now*, Kevin Cann says that three years after my sacking, history kind of repeated itself. As early as 14 April 1973 David and Mick both knew that he was going to break up the Ziggy band live at the Hammersmith Odeon, on 3 July, while the rest of the band were completely in the dark.

At that point, Mick had been offered the opportunity of a glittering solo career guided by MainMan, established by David's manager Tony Defries. This included opportunities of solo recording, touring and the promotion of Mick as a solo artist. The condition was that he 'kept his mouth shut' and didn't jeopardise the success of the *Aladdin Sane* tour by warning others of the impending Ziggy bombshell.

I had barely turned 20 when I was sacked – and some might say I lost out on a dazzling professional career.

Chapter 5
HOMEWARD BOUND

I was devastated to have to leave Haddon Hall next morning, with all my dreams and ambitions shot out of the water. I had to drive all the way back to Hull on my own to face my fiancée and family with as much dignity as I could muster and think about whether to rejoin civilian life or pick up my career back in Hull. I was owed money for sessions at Trident which I was promised would be sent on by cheque, but all I had to my name was a few coppers and the £5 David had lent me to get back to Hull.

David had said I didn't have to go straightaway, but after a miserable evening spent on my own at the local pub, I woke up early and loaded up my drums, clothes and bags into the car ready to leave at 8.30 the next morning. I shared a room with Mick and Roger, and despite all the banging and noise I made, no one got up to help me.

Mick kept his face to the wall throughout.

David and Angie, Tony and Liz were in different rooms and wouldn't have heard me leave anyway – but the way I was feeling, if any of them had got up and offered to help I would have probably told them to fuck off.

I began the route to Hull back through London from Beckenham via Notting Hill and up the Edgware Road to the M1.

My dad, always an unexpected source of wisdom, had once asked: 'Why is it all the Premium Bond winners seem to come from Kent?' – to which nobody had an intelligent answer.

So, feeling lucky (ha, ha!), I decided I would use the change from the £5 to buy a couple of Premium Bonds, and stopped at Kensington Church Street Post Office to buy two of them for £2.

The Premium Bond John bought on the way home after being sacked on the 7 April 1970

I didn't look at these properly for years, but the stamp in the circle has a really strange sequence of letters and numbers. It looks like '7 Apr I O BOW8' (the 8 looks like an E), and when I saw it for the first time I thought it said IO BOWIE (I owe Bowie).

Needless to say, I've kept those Premium Bonds with all my other memorabilia for 50 years now.

I never showed it or mentioned it to David even though he would have appreciated the irony. And guess what? I'm glad I never did, because do you know how much money I have won over the years with those premium bonds?

Fuck all!

At the beginning of the 1970s, Hull still had a thriving fishing industry. There was very little unemployment and plenty of work for a skilled hand. I was an apprentice plasterer and there was plenty of work to be had, while there were also bands and clubs with residencies for musicians.

A couple of weeks after getting back to Hull, I received a very friendly letter and cheque from Tony Visconti, which didn't refer to the sacking at all. He did, however, ask if I could return David the £5 I owed him as he was 'a bit short' at the time!

According to the media, who really hyped up our reunion 19 years later, I would eventually try to return the owed money to David in person.

Anyway, this is the letter Tony sent:

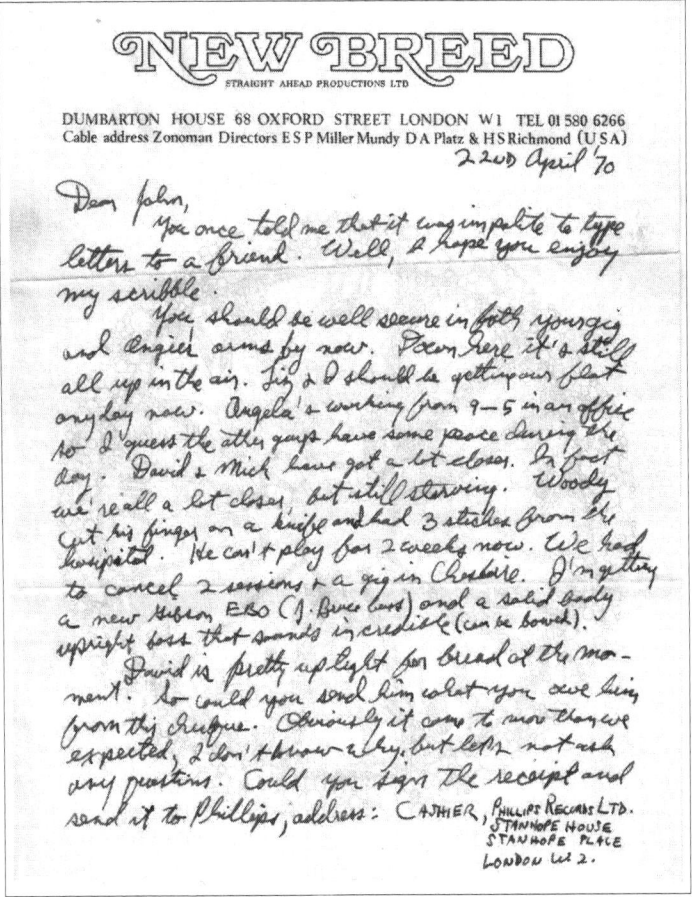

Letter from Tony Visconti (asking for David's fiver back!)

2 —

Send my love to Angie & Mom & Dad. I miss them and if you didn't live so far away I'd be around a lot. Of you wish I will let you know when Jim & I are getting married. Wouldn't want you to miss that.

Hey, I'll be 30 years old in 4 years and two days! How about that? And you'll be thirty in seventeen days and nine years. Don't you feel old?

When I have more time I will add a few chapters to our Fook, Fik legend. Write soon John.

love,

Tony

22 April 1970

Dear John,

You once told me that it was impolite to type a letter to a friend. Well I hope you enjoy my scribble.

You should be well secure in both your gig and Angie's arms by now. Down here it's still all up in the air. Liz and I should be getting our flat any day now, Angela's working from 9–5 in an office so I guess the other guys will have some peace during the day. David and Mick have got a lot closer. In fact we're all a lot closer but still starving. Woody cut his finger on a knife and had three stitches from the hospital. He can't play for two weeks now. We had to cancel two sessions and a gig in Cheshire. I'm getting a new Gibson EBO (Jack Bruce bass) and a solid body upright bass that sounds incredible (can be bowed).

David is pretty uptight for bread at the moment so could you send him what you owe him from the cheque. Obviously it came to more than we expected I don't know why but let's not ask any questions. Could you sign the receipt and send it to Phillips, address: CASHIER , Phillips Records LTD, Stanhope House, Stanhope Place, London W.2

Send my love to Angie & Mam and Dad. I miss them and if you didn't live so far away I'd be round a lot. If you wish I will let you know when Liz and I get married. Wouldn't want you to miss that.

Hey I'll be thirty years old in 4 years and two days! How about that? And you'll be thirty in seventeen days and nine years. Don't you feel old?

When I have more time I will add a few more chapters to our 'Fook, Fack legend'. Write soon John

Love Tony'

The Fook Fak legend Tony mentions was just some daft joke we had about the regional pronunciation of certain expletives (as Dad would say, why use a diminutive word?). In other words, when in Hull, you pronounce the word 'fook' and when from the south 'fak'. That's all, just daft banter.

It was so strange receiving this letter, with its upbeat, conversational tone, as if nothing had happened – for me, everything had happened! – and suggesting that we were all going to continue being friends certainly felt odd to me at the time.

I have since met Tony a couple of times. He would actually go on to marry the singer Mary Hopkin, not Liz, whom I've completely lost touch. It's nice to have known we would have been invited to the wedding though, and as far as Tony was concerned there were no hard feelings.

Just before Christmas 1970 and less than eight months after I had been replaced in Hype, I also received another handwritten letter, this time from Mick himself. He was now back in Hull and reunited with Benny Marshall, Woody and Trevor Bolder in the band Ronno. He and Woody had left David to come back to Hull, with a view to either reforming The Rats (Benny had been contacted by Mick in June 1970, apparently) or possibly starting a new group.

What had happened? Well, The Man Who Sold the World had not enabled David to break through as anticipated and both Mick and Woody became disillusioned – with London, with David and with the fact that instant stardom hadn't followed.

Money was short at Haddon Hall (as Tony says), and as nothing appeared to be happening now, the official story was that they dumped David on the way to a gig up North.

According to Woody, they were driving up to a Hype gig in Leeds and 'forked off' at the split in the M18 for Leeds/Hull, leaving David to do the gig on his own.

Once back in Hull, Mick quickly contacted Benny Marshall, and with Trevor Bolder formed this new group Ronno, releasing a single '4th Hour of My Sleep', which bombed. The record label had lost interest in them without Bowie anyway, so they were left high and dry.

Mick's letter arrived just before Christmas (I haven't the exact date unfortunately).

Hello John,

How are you? I hope that you are O.k. When I've asked people how you are they say that you are pretty settled and happy with your group. I also heard you have a new car. I'm pleased for you.

I felt so embarrassed to get in touch with you. Anyway all I can say is Dave made up his own mind and soon as the l.p. had been finished he threw us out of the house too. And that is why I am home, Anyway

John I wish all the best for Christmas and give our love to your Mam, Dad and Angie wont you.

See you John. Soon perhaps. Mick.

Letter from Mick Ronson

Hello John

How are you ? I hope that you are O.K. When I've asked people how you are they say that you are pretty settled and happy with your group.* I also heard you have a new car. I'm pleased for you.

I felt so embarrassed to get in touch with you. Anyway all I can say is Dave made up his own mind and soon as the LP had been finished he threw us out of the house too, And that is why I am home.

Anyway John I wish you all the best for Christmas and give our love to your Mam, Dad and Angie won't you.

See you John,

Soon perhaps

Mick

*(This must have been The Mandrakes at this time, but without Robert Palmer)

Knowing that he had been a good friend for so many years and had been given the opportunity by me to work with David, I'm not surprised Mick felt a bit 'embarrassed' about getting in touch, especially after he had been the one who had instigated my sacking and replacement with Woody.

At least he tried to reach out, though, but at this point it looked as if it had all gone wrong for him too.

As far as I'm aware, that comment 'David threw us out of the house too' is not quite true, though.

David apparently called Mick again after ten months, when Ronno had failed, to try to tempt him (with Woody and Trevor) back to London. He had now written a collection of amazing new songs, which would eventually become the basis of the *Hunky Dory* and *Ziggy Stardust* albums. In the meantime, he had also got rid of the stigma of being a one-hit wonder when Peter Noone recorded one of his songs 'Oh! You Pretty Things'.

I saw Mick only once more in Hull before he died. Angela and I were walking in Hull city centre near to what was the Cecil Cinema, when he came round the corner with his girlfriend, Denise Irvine. He thrust out his hand, as he always used to, and I shook it, but Angela found it difficult to be friendly and it wasn't a comfortable meeting.

I understand he rarely came back to Hull after he'd finished with Bowie, and to my knowledge it would only have been to visit his family; he never played there again. We didn't speak again until shortly before his death in 1993.

* * *

It was great to see David finally breaking through to the big time, becoming one of the biggest stars in the world. I watched him doing all of the shows we had ever dreamed of doing: *Top of the Pops*, *The Old Grey Whistle Test*, *Russell Harty Plus* and then all the big arena gigs: Ziggy, Serious Moonlight, Glass Spider, Live Aid. He seemed to just go from success to success and be comfortable with the stardom.

Back home I played in various bands over the next few years. I joined The Mandrakes (minus Robert Palmer) and reunited with my old pal John 'Hutch' Hutchinson, that other Bowie alumnus, for quite a few gigs. For some time I also played in a group called Uncle Sam, backing the well-known Country and Western singer Tammy Cline. (I actually wrote and played on a song released as a single on the President label, titled 'I Wish I'd Wrote That Song' – which received national airplay). We supported the Welsh comedian Max Boyce with Tammy and also played Nashville! I had many long-term residencies at various clubs in Hull and the East Riding, where I was finally settled, married and started a family.

I nearly resumed my London career, though, and had a couple of other near misses with big bands over the years. In June 1972 I got a call from one of our old Rats' ex-roadies to tell me that Badfinger needed a drummer and that he had put my name forward. He gave me a number to ring, which I called and was invited to London for an audition. I headed down to Tin Pan Alley, Denmark Street, where the audition was being held in the basement of a small club.

There were other drummers being auditioned when I arrived, so I grabbed a pint and picked up some darts to throw at the board by myself. After a while they had a break from auditions and when

John playing with The Mandrakes at The Lord Mayors Hall in Paris, 1971.
First band since returning home

Tammy Cline & Uncle Sam. L-R Lynn Blakeston, Tammy Cline, John
Cambridge, Rod Boulton, Tony Beasty

the band came upstairs for a drink, I got chatting to one of them and we ended up having a game of darts.

When it was my turn, I was called down into the basement and they asked me if I knew any of Badfinger's numbers. They'd been signed by the Beatles' Apple label, and had recently recorded 'Come and Get It', written and produced by Paul McCartney. They had also just had a hit earlier that year with 'Day After Day', produced by George Harrison. Mal Evans, who if you remember got me those Beatles autographs (we think) all those years ago, had produced the single 'No Matter What', one of Badfinger's other Top 10 hit singles.

They were quite a big name group at the time, great songwriters who also wrote the blockbuster 'Without You', which became a worldwide No. 1 for Harry Nilsson and, later, Mariah Carey. So this was potentially quite a big deal for me, possibly even bigger than Bowie had seemed in 1970–71. The first number I did for them was 'The Weight' by The Band and then a few more songs before their hit 'Day After Day'.

The audition was over and their manager approached me and said: 'I think I should let you know it's not a permanent role. It's to do an American tour, as their permanent drummer didn't want it. Are you still interested?' I said: 'Yes' and he said: 'Good, I'll contact you in a few days with all the details.'

A few days later I got the call – but, as often seems to happen, their drummer had changed his mind and had now agreed to do the whole US tour.

It seems I was spared by not working with Badfinger, however, as they eventually got into all sorts of financial and professional trouble and two of the band ended up taking their own lives.

A similar brush with the big time happened in January 1975 with the former Amen Corner lead singer, Andy Fairweather-Lowe, who was about to have a big solo hit in December of that same year with 'Wide-Eyed and Legless'. My name was suggested when his band said he would be looking for a drummer. This was after Hutch and I had appeared with him on the Tyne Tees Television programme *The Geordie Scene*. I was asked for an audition, only to be told later that Henry Spinetti had been recruited before it could even happen.

'Hutch and It's Easy' at Tyne Tees studio's Newcastle, 1975. Appearing on the TV Programme called *The Geordie Scene*

Whenever people asked: 'Is it true you played drums for David Bowie?', I would reply, 'Oh yes, and the Beatles and Elvis, Frank Sinatra and …', always trying to play it down a bit. I could have just flashed the autograph book, I suppose, which contained the signatures of nearly every big name I'd worked with and which really is a Who's Who of '60s and '70s Rock and Roll.

In 1976 my wife Angela was selling a pram and put an advert in the *Hull Daily Mail*. A couple from the village of Paull, just outside of Hull, came to look at it with a view to buy.

My drum cases were stacked high in our hallway, ready to take to a gig. When he saw them, the man whipped out his wallet and flashed a photograph, saying: 'Do you know who that is?'

I said I did, it was Dave Hill, the lead guitarist from Slade.

'That's her brother,' he said proudly nodding to his wife. 'There you go. I thought you might be impressed.'

I didn't say anything.

You see I've never shouted out that I'd been David Bowie's drummer or his best man or bragged about all of the big names I've worked with over the years. I know some people might be quick to cash in on reflected glory, but that's not me. However, sometimes people tip the press off and I get called by newspapers and radio for comments on Bowie and all things related. I even get invited to contribute to documentaries like *Five Years*, *Besides Bowie* and *Passions*. Until this book, I have never really put much of this into any formal words.

Maybe that's another reason David and I stayed friends. I never cashed in on my time with him by spilling the beans about any secrets and scandals. I even took a lot of persuading to write all this down (as I said before, for the most part I couldn't be arsed). I never thought what I'd achieved was worth writing about more than my dad's war exploits.

I always admired modesty, especially my dad's. He never talked about his war adventures with any conceit and I've always respected people who are genuinely talented or might have good reason to brag about their achievements but don't. Over the years I have played with or supported many fantastic artists and have been a fan of lots more, especially drummers like myself, whom I have admired from afar and who choose to keep a more grounded and balanced profile.

In 1982 we took a family holiday to visit Angela's other brother Allen in East Dereham, Norfolk, just ten miles from Scoulton, where I'd rehearsed with Junior's Eyes 13 years before. We stayed until the following Wednesday before heading off to London at the invitation of one of my good mates at the time, John Hawley. John was a professional footballer who had played for Hull City, Leeds United and Sunderland but was currently at Arsenal and living in a house in Highgate provided by them. I had stayed there while gigging with Tammy Cline on several occasions previously. We arrived around teatime, just as John was about to leave to play in a charity cricket match for Arsenal and he asked me along to come and watch. As it was pouring down, the cricket match was postponed, so we stayed in the clubhouse for a drink and a game of pool with Graham Rix and Alan Sunderland, who both came from Yorkshire too.

While standing at the bar, John pointed to somebody who I thought was the barman, generally tidying up and wiping tables. 'Clem's a drummer,' he said. Immediately, my ears pricked up. *Wait a minute, Clem's not a common name*, I thought. So I asked him: 'What's your surname, Clem?' and he replied: 'Cattini.'

'Not *the* Clem Cattini, the session drummer?'

'Yes,' he said.

'Do you realise who this man is?' I said to John. 'He's played on stacks of hit records. He's an absolute legend!'

It turned out that Clem was also a massive Arsenal fan and happily gave his time freely for any charitable endeavours. Clem has played on over 40 No. 1 hit records, including Dusty Springfield's 'You Don't Have to Say you Love Me', 'Shaking all Over' by Johnny Kidd & the Pirates, 'All Day and All of the Night' by The Kinks, 'Hot Love' by T. Rex, 'The Sun Ain't Gonna Shine Anymore' and 'Make it Easy on Yourself' by The Walker Brothers, 'Hi Ho Silver Lining' by Jeff Beck and The Tornados 'Telstar'.

I immediately got Clem to give me an autograph.

I had managed to get every autograph in that book in person (apart from the Beatles), which must give the collection extra authenticity. As you can see, there are some famous names in that book, including Jimi Hendrix who even told me I should 'stay kool'. By contrast I even got a signed photo of Bernard Manning who wrote the word 'Twat' (typical) after we'd backed him.

But I never got David's! I was never to play on stage with David again but my association with him was by no means over.

Chapter 6
REUNITED

It was to be nearly 20 years before I actually met David again, at St George's Hall, Bradford and a lot of water had passed under the bridge in the time between.

He was playing there with his band Tin Machine on Sunday, 2 July 1989, and I was playing a residency at Hull's Ritz Club at the same time. I played at the Ritz for four years, until June 1992, and then did seven months as landlord at the Swallow on Bransholme before I eventually became landlord of the Forrester's Arms in Beverley.

This is all relevant, as you'll see later in the story.

On Saturday, 1 July 1989, I had a phone call from Viking Radio in Hull to ask if I would go into the studio for an interview. It was to be about David's new band, Tin Machine, and the Bradford concert the next day (Sunday).

The week before, a West Yorkshire newspaper had rung to ask if I would be going to see David at the gig. I told them of course it would be nice to meet up again but I had no plans to at that point. They also somehow knew about the fiver I'd borrowed from David to get back to Hull.

The Viking Radio presenter asked me if it was true that I was going to 'meet David and give him back the fiver that I owe him.' So I said, 'No. I have no plans to go to Bradford. In fact, I'll be at work plastering that day.' I had no idea how they had found out about the money.

I went to work that day as usual. For a self-employed plasterer, Sunday is just another working day. While there I tuned in to Viking FM, and noticed they kept mentioning the Tin Machine gig and the fact that I was supposedly going to present the fiver back to David 'on stage', in front of the packed audience. This was just getting silly.

After hearing this repeated on local radio all morning, I started to think, *Maybe I should give it a try*.

I hadn't seen David in person since 1970. We'd spoken a couple of times on the phone while he was still at Haddon Hall, but that was it.

Maybe this was an opportunity to reach out and reconnect. Would I even be able to get to him? How would he be with me after all these years?

I knew I had to at least try, so I left work early to go back home, change and tell Angela that I was off to Bradford. I then rang Graham 'Grom' Kelly, the former singer from Junior's Eyes, who lived in Bradford and who I'd also kept in touch with, to see if he fancied coming along too.

We'd exchanged the odd Christmas card and phone call over the years and he said he'd like to go, but I had a problem.

I was still resident drummer at the Ritz Club in Hull along with my good mate Lynn 'Blako' Blakeston. I rang Blako before I left to see if he could get a deputy drummer that night and told him what I was trying to do. He agreed to do his best to help and put my mind at rest; I hate letting people down.

I met Grom at the stage door in Bradford at about 2 o'clock and asked the security staff if David had arrived yet.

No, was the answer, so we headed to the nearest bar, which was in the hotel opposite St George's Hall. While we were sitting there enjoying a drink somebody shouted, 'Is there a John Cambridge here?'

'Yes,' I said, 'here.'

'It's your wife'.

Bloody hell, I thought, *she's tracked me down already!*

'How did you know I was here, Sherlock?' I said.

'It wasn't difficult,' she replied. 'I just rang directory enquiries and asked them for the telephone number of the nearest bar to St George's Hall. I knew that's where you'd be! Anyway, I was right, wasn't I?'

Angela said that Blako had rung her to say he couldn't get a stand-in after all, but not to worry; under the circumstances, they could manage for the night. After some time reminiscing, Grom and I went back to the stage door where fans were now gathering. David still hadn't arrived. Back and forth, between pub and stage door, we went until about 5.30, when Grom said he was fed up of hanging around, he was going home. I didn't blame him.

I waited another half-hour and thought I'd give it *one last try, and if David isn't there, I'm going back home too.* All sorts of thoughts and doubts were now going through my mind, including the fear that I was being fobbed off. Back at the stage door there were even more fans now but also someone who looked like a stage manager at the entrance talking to them. I pushed through and asked again if David had arrived yet.

'Yes,' he said. 'They're just about to do a soundcheck.'

'Can you get a message to him?' I said, but not hopeful. 'Can you tell him that an old friend, John Cambridge, is outside and would like to see him. If he's busy or he hasn't got time, I'll understand.'

He went inside, came straight back out and waved me over. 'Come in,' he said.

I was beginning to feel really nervous now, and was taken backstage where I sat on a huge flight case. Tin Machine had already started their soundcheck and I thought they were tight, good, but loud, even though there was a wall separating me from the stage.

A young drummer had started to assemble his drum kit in front of me. He told me his band had won a competition by drawing lots to see who could support Tin Machine. I think he must have assumed I was one of the road crew.

After about 20 minutes of listening to the soundcheck and chatting to this young lad, the music stopped. My eyes were now focused on the gap at the back of the stage and I saw David walk past, double back and then walk straight towards me.

I hadn't seen him for almost 20 years!

I jumped off the flight case as he approached. 'John!' he said and gave me great big hug. 'How are you, how are you doing? It's great to see you.' And now this drummer, setting up his gear, had nearly fallen over in amazement.

David stood back with his hands on his hips. 'Now what's all this about a fiver?' he asked, holding out his hand and smiling. He'd obviously been listening to local radio or somebody had tipped him off too!

'Well, David, you know what the media are like! Nothing to do with me,' I replied.

I'd brought my little Instamatic camera and asked the poor gobsmacked drummer if he would take a photo of David and me, which he did.

I also had my treasured autograph book with me this time and told David about how, when I was working on building sites, people used to sometimes ask: 'Is it true you used to play drums for David Bowie?'

If it was somebody who wanted to pump me for the full story, I had to watch that the plaster on the walls didn't set before I'd finished telling them, so I used to fob them off with that stock answer: 'Oh yes and with Elvis and Frank Sinatra too.'

Then they thought I was probably not serious and stopped pestering. When I handed David the autograph book, he started looking through it and noticed my signed photo of Johnny Kidd & the Pirates. He said, 'Oh we've just started doing "Shaking all Over" by them, but I don't know all the lyrics. Do you know the second verse, John?'

I did, and wrote them out for him, reminding him how it went. But then he said, 'Do you know the drum break in the middle?' He meant the famous Clem Cattini drum break, which fortunately I also knew how to play. (I think it might have been in the early *Beano* annual repertoire too.)

I tapped it out on my knees when he called his drummer over. Why I didn't just do it on the drummer's snare in front of me I'll never know – maybe I was nervous or maybe it was memories of another tricky drum fill I was asked to play all those years ago. I couldn't help thinking, *How strange is this that I'm showing Bowie's drummer how to play this after all that had happened?'*

After I'd told him some of the building sites stories, I handed him the autograph book to sign, and he started laughing as he was writing. I thought, *He's taking a long time just to sign his name.* When he handed it back to me, I could see why.

He'd written: 'For John, it was nice to meet you, but please stop

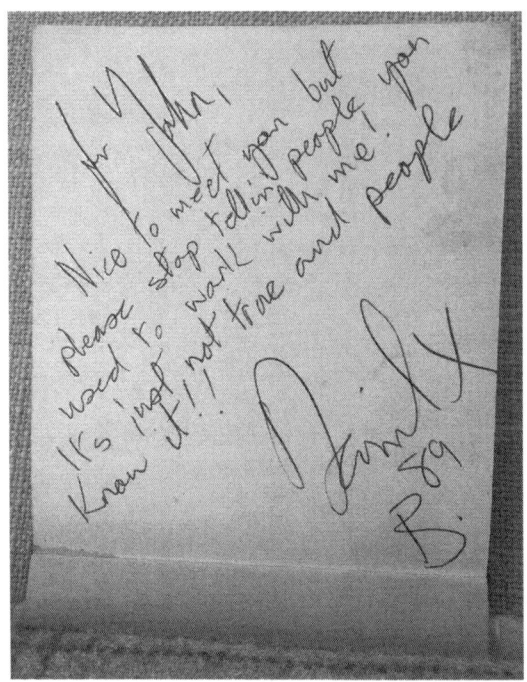

Bowie autograph at the Tin Machine gig, 1989

telling people you used to work with me! It's just not true and they know it!! David x '89 B'

I mentioned his hair, which was a lot shorter than the last time we'd been together (long and permy compared to my own thinning thatch).

'Yes, you've always had a good head of hair,' I said. 'Bastard'.

He laughed and mimicked my accent, like he always used to. 'Bah stood,' he said. He'd seen and done some amazing things since we'd last met and been through some dark and dangerous times. He was now regarded as one of the most important recording artists of the twentieth century, but for me he still had the same boyish sense of humour – and we seemed to just carry on from where we'd left it all those years ago.

'Have you got any tickets for tonight's show?' he asked.

'No', I replied, at which point he waved his fingers at the stage manager who happened to be passing and said: 'Can you get me two comps for John, please?'

I didn't have the guts to tell him I was supposed to be playing in the Ritz Club back in Hull that night. I began to feel guilty about that. After collecting the comps, I went back with him to the dressing room and asked for a number to keep in touch. He said that he was living in Switzerland, but that he was only there for about three months a year so he wouldn't give me that number which was a landline.

'I'll give you my secretary Eileen's number. I speak to her every day, so if you call her, she'll pass it on straightaway. Have you got anything to write it on?'

The only thing I had on me was one of my plastering business cards and that's what he wrote the number on. We then said our goodbyes (for now) and I went back to my car leaving David with the promise we'd stay in touch.

It was now 7 o'clock and I was thinking about my old mate Blako back at The Ritz, drummerless, so I set off back for Hull.

I arrived back at the Ritz about half an hour late, but just in time to back the guest guitar-vocalist with his set. The first number was 'Ten Guitars' by Englebert Humperdinck and I just played along with it, the loud sound of Tin Machine still ringing in my ears.

Back to the real world, eh?

Someone from Hull who was at the Tin Machine concert told me David had asked for me by name on stage and even tried to locate me in the audience.

But now my contact with David was re-established, and a lot of the hurt had gone.

There's a great scene in the film *Yesterday* when the singer Jack Malik, played by Himesh Patel, wakes up in a parallel universe where the Beatles never existed. He becomes famous playing all of their big hits, but then goes to meet John Lennon, who in this version of history hasn't even become a singer and has lived safely as a result until the age of 78 – a completely different, happy life.

I'll never know if I had become one of the Spiders from Mars whether the lovely family I have around me now would even exist, whether I was cut out for that kind of glitz and glamour and the sacrifices that went with it.

It was great to feel that David and I were back in touch, though, and that something which had devastated me at the time had in some ways been addressed.

The *Hull Daily Mail* reported on 'Bowie and old friend in reunion' two days later and I went back to my proper job, though

Bowie and old friend in reunion

By MAIL REPORTER

HULL-BASED drummer John Cambridge last night had a reunion with pop superstar David Bowie 20 years to the month since he was first in his backing band.

John (40), of Arden Road, Beverley, was in Bowie's band The Hype when he first made the charts with Space Oddity.

He was also at Bowie's wedding to his ex-wife Angie and then introduced him to Hull guitarist Mick Ronson, who led Bowie's band the Spiders from Mars as he shot to world fame.

But John had not met Bowie since 1970 until last night's 20-minute reunion before his sell-out concert at St Georges Hall, Bradford.

Bowie offered John tickets for the concert but he turned them down to dash back to fulfil his residency at Hull's Ritz Club!

Helped

But Bowie still gave him his private number in New York and some autographs and they had a set of photographs taken together. In return, John even helped Bowie with his stage act.

"He saw a picture of Johnny Kidd in my autograph book and said that they were doing Shakin' All Over in the show, but he knew only the first verse," said John.

"So I ended up going through the drum break with his drummer from the Tin Machine and writing the second verse on the back of my business card as a plasterer!"

And he added: "Bowie was ever so friendly and it was nice to talk about the old days. He was even laughing about my Hull accent just as he always used to.

"And whatever some people might think about him, he's still the same person he was when I left him all that time ago — a really good kid."

Hull Daily Mail article, 1989. Reunion with Bowie at the Tin Machine gig

David and I now spoke more regularly and communicated through letter and email too.

In 1993 my wife and I were running the Forrester's Arms pub in Beverley. On Wednesday, 10 March, I was busy upstairs when my daughter Adele shouted from the downstairs phone: 'Dad, there's David Bowie on the phone for you.' It was, and he was ringing from Switzerland.

After we'd chatted a while he got round to the reason he'd called. 'Have you heard that Mick's got cancer?'

I said I'd heard rumours but didn't know how bad it was. I'd tried to get a contact number from Mick's mother Minnie, who was still living in the same house on Greatfield Estate where Mick had grown up in, but she said: 'Michael doesn't want to be bothered by people' and wouldn't give it to me.

So David said, 'Well, I have, I'll give you it.

'He just won't stop smoking his bloody roll-ups,' he added.

I told him I hadn't spoken to Mick for over 20 years and that we'd lost touch. I'd followed his career, but that was it, we'd both gone on different paths and didn't really have a lot in common any more.

I got Mick's number from Bowie and in return gave him Stuey's, his old bodyguard/minder.

I sat on the number for four days, but then, on the Sunday at about 11.30, I thought *Shall I give Mick a ring? Maybe I should.* We were all night owls in those days and nobody in my circle would have complained about receiving a phone call at that time, so I rang the London number. It went straight to answerphone.

'I'm sorry, I'm not available at the moment,' the message said.

I said: 'Hello, it's John Cambridge here. I'm an old friend just ringing to see how Mick is' and I left my number.

I didn't hold out much hope that Mick would actually get back to me.

A few minutes later my phone rang. It was Mick, just as pleased to hear from me as I was from him, and we talked and laughed and joked about all sorts – about The Rats and gigs we'd done, people we knew. Neither of us mentioned the cancer.

I said, 'You still come back to Hull to see your mum, don't you?' He said yes, so I said: 'Well look, next time you do we'll get together and have a really good catch-up, or if you like I'll come down to London and we'll do the same.'

'Yes', he said, 'I'll really look forward to that.'

Sadly, that meeting never took place.

Kevin Cann told me later that Mick had always really wanted to get in touch but hesitated to call because he wasn't sure what my reaction would be. Mick's liver cancer was terminal and he must have been in a lot of pain and discomfort, despite the brave public face he always put on. He was receiving chemotherapy treatment in London, which was making him ill. He was pale and gaunt but still working and had recently produced Morrisey's album *Your Arsenal*. Just months before he died he played at the Freddie Mercury tribute concert, his last ever live gig, and to a global audience, with David Bowie and Ian Hunter.

I wrote to Mick too and sent him a letter full of daft jokes to cheer him up. His sister Maggi said later he really appreciated it.

In his book *Bowie & Hutch*, Hutch said that he thought Mick's liver cancer might have been made worse by heavy drinking, the rock and roll lifestyle. This was the young lad who would get tipsy and daft after just one pint.

On 29 April 1993 he died of liver cancer in a house on Hasker Street in Chelsea, London. He is now buried in Hull's Eastern Cemetery near to Greatfied Estate, where his family lived and where he grew up.

It was a sad thing to see his decline. On the day he died, Ched Cheesman called me to tell me the news, followed a bit later by Bowie himself who, like me, didn't really know what to say.

I went to his memorial in London and then back to the house in Hasker Street, where he had died the week before. I met Ian Hunter who said Mick had told him a lot about me. One of the saddest things I remember was going upstairs to the bathroom toilet and seeing Mick's shaving things all laid out the sink, untouched since he'd died. I was one of only a handful of friends from Hull to go, including Ian 'Gibbo' Gibson, Stuey George and my wife, Angela.

I was to take part in several tributes to Ronno over the coming years, including most recently *Turn and Face the Strange* by Garry Burnett and Rupert Creed, the show which tells the story of Mick's career and rise to fame. I play drums in the show band and tell some of the stories from this book live.

How different for all of us it might have been if I'd never gone back to seek him out to play in Hype, that time when he was gardening and marking pitches by day and playing evenings in The Rats. If Mick had stayed in Hull and I had been the one to stay in London, all our lives, including David's, would have probably taken a completely different course.

We'll just never know.

* * *

On Monday 23 September 1997 a FedEx van pulled up outside our house in Beverley. Royal Mail vans were a familiar sight, but we'd never before had a FedEx delivery and we were curious. The driver handed me a cardboard box approximately five inches thick by a foot and a half square. After I'd signed for it, I noticed it had been sent from New York.

There was only one person I knew who lived there – David.

It weighed nothing and when I shook it, there seemed to be nothing inside. 'Somebody's sent us an empty box, all the way from New York,' I said to Angela.

'Come on, open it and see,' she said.

Inside was a letter from David's wife Iman.

I felt really honoured that I would be included in this, even after all these years. I knew then that he still valued me as a friend, which mattered a lot. I couldn't help wondering what David must have told Iman about our time together in Hype and how much our friendship had meant to him for her to know so much about me. Iman asked me to write (not print or type) a few pages about any memories I had of David and send any photos of us together. I did this and included a photo that Tony Visconti had sent me from the Haddon Hall days of us playing football in the grounds. Putting all of these things back into the box (I knew now why it had been posted empty), I sent it back to New York on 15 October 1996.

As we were approaching Christmas, I just mentioned to Angela, 'I wonder if we might get an invite to his 50th birthday party?'

Shortly after, we received a lovely hand-coloured (by David) invitation! I thought at first the party might have been in London,

I MAN™

September 18 , 1996

Mr. John Cambridge

ENGLAND

Dear John:

I am writing to you in the hopes that you will participate in my birthday present to David for his 50th birthday. I am putting together a book of which there will be only one copy (for him) with letters or testaments from his family and friends saying what he has meant to each of them over the years. I know how much you have meant to David and how much it would mean to me to include you in this very personal gift.

Because of the printer's deadlines, I would need your contribution returned by November 1, 1996 to the following address:

Needless to say, David does not know about this and I would like to surprise him so I am hoping we can keep this a secret!

My warmest regards,

Iman Bowie

135 EAST 55TH STREET, 6TH FLOOR, NEW YORK, NY 10022. TEL: 212.750.6776. FAX: 212.750.2279

Letter from Iman Bowie asking for John's contribution to her special book, a gift to David for his 50th birthday

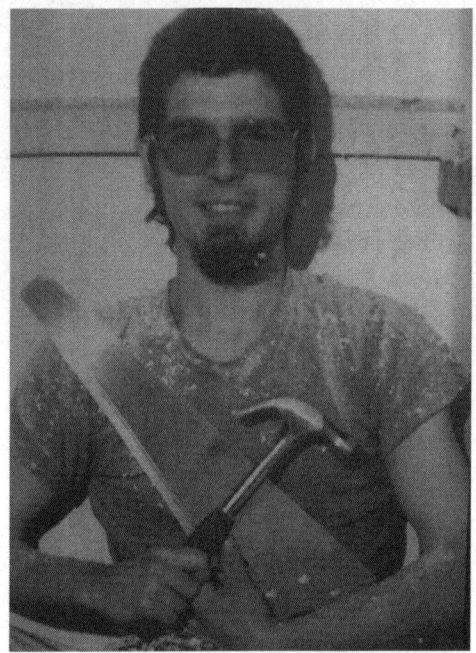

Tony helping to create Ziggy Sawdust!

which would have been much easier to reach and affordable, but no, it was in New York!

At the time Angela and I were still paying off a debt to the brewery after leaving the pub trade, and there was no way we could have afforded a trip to New York. I was playing drums at the Springhead pub in Anlaby every Thursday with my two good mates Pete Alison and Brian Farr in a duo called Distinction. Terry Kent, the landlord of Springhead offered to lend me £500, which he would deduct from my weekly fee. Really nice of him, but it still wouldn't have been enough, so we were resigned to staying at home.

Early in the New Year Lorraine rang from Iman Bowie's office to ask if we could confirm if we were coming to the party. It was with a heavy heart I had to tell her no.

That night, Angela and I went out to drown our sorrows at the Cross Keys, the pub owned by our friends, Brian and Sharon

Brookes. I was doing some plastering for Brian at his other property next door at the time and Angela was working as a cook in a nursery for two of our other friends, Tim and Carol. We all sat down together to have a drink.

When the conversation eventually came around to Bowie's 50th birthday party, we had to explain why we weren't going. On hearing this, both couples very generously said that they would lend us £500 each and that we could work it off our wages, me by plastering and Angela at the nursery on condition that they come with us too.

Sharon booked the flights and I immediately rang Eileen at David's office to tell her that we'd changed our minds, we would be there after all.

We arrived in New York on 8 January 1997, the day of David's 50th birthday. The party was to be the next day after a concert by him at Madison Square Gardens. We booked into the Pennsylvania Hotel, directly opposite the venue and where Glenn Miller had played a residency The hotel's phone number inspired the song 'Pennsylvania 6-5000'.

I had to collect the six complimentary tickets for the gig from the Bowie office and two VIP passes for Angela and myself. Also on the bill were Robert Smith, The Foo Fighters, Lou Reed, Frank Black, Sonic Youth and Billy Corgan. The evening was billed as 'David Bowie and Friends – A Very Special Birthday Celebration' and all of the above musical friends were to join him at some point on stage, including Lou Reed for a special extended set.

We all took our seats, and Angela and I went to see the bar for which we'd been given VIP passes. It was empty, so we just had a quick look around it and then came back to our seats. Brian asked me could he just borrow the passes, so he and Sharon could go and have a look too.

He not only went in and got himself a complimentary bottle of Budweiser but then went and put his 'Cross Keys' pub business cards on every table. I mean, honestly, who is going to pick up a card in a bar in Manhattan and think, *Oh, that's useful, I'll keep this handy just in case I'm looking for a cheap B&B in East Yorkshire?*

Bowie's latest album played loudly over the P.A. system as we were waiting for the show to start and as I wondered which artist would open the show. The lights went out and the track 'Little

Wonder' came blasting out even louder than the rest of the album. The arena was pitch-black with just the track playing when the stage lights suddenly came up, dazzling bright – and there he was, David, singing the song live.

It was so good I honestly thought at first it was the recording, and the audience went wild.

Then other friends joined David for various duets, including Lou Reed on 'Queen Bitch' and 'Waiting for the Man' and Robert Smith on 'Quicksand'. It was an amazing concert, culminating in an incredible version of 'Space Oddity' with David right out on the catwalk playing a 12-string guitar. The whole thing can be seen on YouTube.

Angie and I quickly dashed across the road to the hotel afterwards to get changed for the party. We thought we'd better get there early, and before David arrived if possible, just in case it was a surprise. We took a yellow cab to an address in Greenwich Village, which we later discovered was the house of a famous Hollywood actor, and arrived at about 11.20 pm. Parked outside was a blue and white NYPD police car, with barriers around the doorway and flanked by a doorman and security guard. There were already photographers waiting to catch the arrival of celebrity guests. Unsurprisingly, they didn't all rush to photograph us.

I approached the security man with the invitation in my hand, trying all the time to keep it in pristine condition (see the photograph) – but he didn't even look at it when I showed him. (I suppose documents can always be forged.) 'What's your name, buddy?' he asked and pulled a list out of his pocket. That's when I noticed he was carrying a gun.

'Yeah, you're on the list, you can go in.'

We entered the huge multistorey building, turned down a corridor, and then left into a garage with a large black Mercedes limousine covered in dust.

'I don't think it's here,' I said, as we turned back into the corridor. Suddenly the wall appeared to open in front of us, revealing one of those elevators where the top slides up and the bottom half goes down, the kind I've only ever seen on American TV programmes. There were chairs down either side and another huge bodyguard acting as lift operator, also carrying a gun.

'Two coming up,' he said into an intercom as we travelled all the way to the top. The doors then opened into a large, very dimly lit room which looked like an artist's studio; there were many of his covered-up canvases leaning against the walls, draped with sheets. The room had about twenty-five round tables which seated eight people each, set in five rows and with a candle burning in the middle of each one.

Eerie mood music was playing and we were approached straight-away by a smart young waiter carrying a tray of wine-filled glasses. We each took one glass and sat in a far corner.

Apart from the waiters, we were the only ones there for a while, but the room slowly started to fill up. Then, about an hour later, we heard a round of applause as David and Iman arrived. There were speeches, which were then followed by the unveiling of a painting – a birthday present, I think, to David from Iman.

There was to be no dancing or singing and everybody sat down, eating food from the buffet and drinking. We were still the only ones on our table, maybe because we were a bit out of the way, but I could clearly see David getting a lot of attention from various guests, as you would expect on your 50th birthday, and his table was right in the middle of the room.

I thought I'd better wait until the attention had died down a bit and then go over to see him, but the queue never subsided, and as soon as somebody left him, somebody else had jumped in and taken their place. I began to wonder if I would actually get to talk to David that night and whether he would even know I was there.

In the meantime, we carried on enjoying the wine and dis-creetly spotting celebrity guests like Christopher Walken, who came over to our corner for a smoke. Naomi Campbell walked by, and we guessed she was probably a friend of Iman's.

I noticed Iman walking towards us behind the tables. (Remem-ber, we were on the back row in a corner.) I thought it was time to make a move, so I got up and approached her. She obviously wouldn't know who I was, so as we met I said, 'Hi, Iman, I'm John Cambridge –' Before I could finish, she interrupted me and grabbed my hand.

'John! You made it!' she said, which immediately sent me into a complete daze.

'Have you spoken to David yet? Come on.' And she led me straight to David's table, where he had his back to us, talking to someone. Iman tapped him on the shoulder and when he didn't respond, she started to give him a little neck massage which made him turn around to see us, jump up and shout 'John!', while giving me a big hug.

I wished him a Happy Birthday and thanked him for the invitation. Then we just seemed to pick up from where we'd left off before and started to talk and laugh about all sorts – family, mutual friends, etc.

Eventually I went back to Angela and then to the toilet. We were in someone's house (a very big house), remember, so the toilet was in the bathroom and there was a bit of a queue forming outside the door. I noticed that the person in front of me was Reeves Gabrels, the guitarist who had just played at Madison Square Gardens with David, so I told him I'd really enjoyed the show and in return he was really interested to know that I used to be in Hype with David and Mick Ronson.

Then it was Reeves' turn. I went in after he'd finished, and when I came out he was still there, waiting for me, in order to carry on the conversation. I felt honoured that he wanted to know all about my time playing in bands with David and Ronno, and especially the early Hype days.

Here goes my impostor syndrome again, worrying whether I was worthy of a seat at this table and thinking that it should have been the other way round – me waiting to ask Reeves about his glittering career.

Unbeknown to me, Angela had gone to see David while I was chatting to Reeves and asked if she could get a photo of us together. He still remembered her and said: 'Angela, give me a minute and I'll be over'. A few minutes later I noticed him walking straight towards us. 'Right then, where's this camera?' he said.

I hadn't seen many photos taken that night, though there had been a couple of photographers around. They must have seen this as a cue to begin taking photos as David posed with me.

Angela took us with our arms round each other, 'standing by the wall' as flashes from the other photographers' cameras added extra light to the picture in that really dark room.

That's the photo we have used for the cover of this book.

When I did eventually go back to David and Iman's table, I saw another friend from the past – George Underwood. George was the person who thumped David in the eye all those years ago and caused his pupil to be permanently dilated. He became a painter and did some fantastic artwork for David's albums.

He and David were still really good friends too, despite the eye!

Angela came to get a photo of George and myself, which David photobombed – and which actually turned out quite nice, relaxed and natural looking!

* * *

I continued to hear more regularly from David, though we only actually got together face to face every five or so years. He sent me a big magnum of champagne on my 50th birthday and we corresponded by email, Christmas card and the occasional phone call. I even invited him to my daughter Adele's wedding sometime later, which he and Iman graciously declined.

One night in September 2002 we went for a drink in Beverley and our last port of call was the Dog and Duck, a pub right next to the Beverley Playhouse, the former cinema which had also been a fantastic concert venue in the '90s and early '2000s. Appearing there that night were the hit '70s band The Strawbs, and my old mate Steve Trice and Rick Kemp were both in the pub having a drink and waiting to be joined by Dave Cousins, the lead singer. Rick, you might remember from earlier in the book, was formerly the bassist for Steeleye Span and Michael Chapman, who also ran the music department in Hammonds, Hull in the '60s.

When Dave finally came, I reminded him that I'd played a gig with Bowie at his pub, the White Bear in Hounslow, in 1970. I think he was even more surprised that I'd remembered the name of the pub rather than the gig. He asked if I was going to see David at the Hammersmith Apollo the following week, but as I didn't know anything about it, I said I very much doubted it. When we got home, I thought it would be nice to keep the contact with David going, so I called Eileen at the office in New York to see what was possible. The office then rang back straightaway to say there were two tickets and backstage passes waiting at the box office if we wanted them.

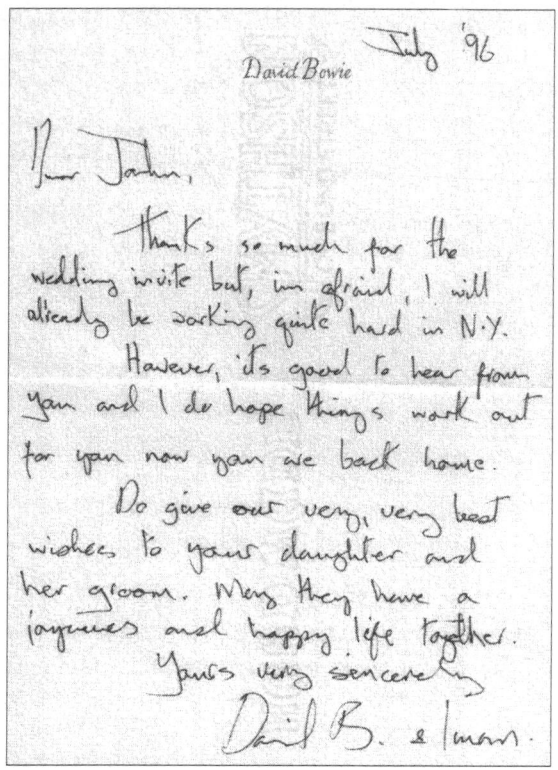

David Bowie   July '96

Dear John,

thanks so much for the wedding invite but, im afraid, I will already be working quite hard in N.Y.

However, its good to hear from you and I do hope things work out for you now you are back home.

Do give out very, very best wishes to your daughter and her groom. May they have a joyness and happy life together.

Yours very sincerely

David B. s/man.

David's reply letter to John's daughter's wedding invite

On 2 October, Angela and I got the train to London and booked into a Holiday Inn within easy walking distance of the venue. We got to the box office about 6 p.m. to collect the comps and then met George Underwood, his wife and son at the upstairs bar at the venue. At this point, I finally had acquired a brick-sized mobile phone and was able to liaise with George easily.

David was on stage at 8.15, and about halfway through the show I went out to get couple more drinks to take inside the theatre. I expected the bar to be empty, as everyone was watching the show and guessed I could probably get served and back really quickly. Standing at the bar was none other than Boy George (plus friend), dressed in a flowery hat and suit. Now George is supposed to be an uber Bowie fan and apparently has a *Mastermind* knowledge about Bowie's career, especially the early years.

I was sorely tempted to go over and say, *Excuse me, George. I understand you know a lot about David's history?* – and follow up with *Can you tell me who the first drummer was in Hype?*

But I didn't – anymore than I play the game of 'my celebrity mate is bigger than your celebrity mate.'

It was a funny thought, though!

There was no queue at the merchandise stall, so just like a regular punter I went and bought a Bowie poster for £5.

The show finished about 10.45 and we went back to the upstairs bar, where you now had to show your passes. I noticed Roger Taylor of Queen standing at the bar having a drink and heard someone shout 'Cambo!'. I looked round to see another old Hull friend, Gary Miller, who is a top guitarist and producer (just Google him).

'What are you doing here?' I asked.

'I've just produced Bowie's new single "Everyone Says Hi",' he replied.

'I thought Tony Visconti did that?' I said.

'No, Tony passed a tape of David singing it with just a 12-string guitar. I added drums, keyboard and lead guitar.'

Getting to see David was like booking an audience with the Pope. Even George Underwood was told it was only two at a time for his ten-minute slot, forcing his wife to hang back when he and his son went through. I can understand how it could easily end up with David being trapped there all night if people kept talking with no limit on their time.

'Where is he, anyway? I can't see him?' I said, when we finally got to the room where the audience was taking place. Then I noticed him talking to a group of people and every ten minutes or so a lady, who I think was Coco Schwab (David's PA), came up and very politely asked if they would finish and move on.

When it was our turn, David gave me his usual big hug and Angela a kiss. He told me that he had stopped smoking since his daughter Lexi has been born. He always used to have a packet of Marlboro Lights in his hand.

I asked him, 'You do know who brought tobacco to this country?'

'Walter Raleigh,' he replied.

'What else did he bring back at the same time?' I asked.

'Potatoes,' he said.

'Correct,' I said, 'but what would have happened if he'd got them mixed up? We could have been carrying big sacks over our shoulders, saying "Here, light me one up" or "Have one of mine",' which made him laugh.

'Do you realise David, that since 1970 we have met in person, on average every seven years,' I said. 'I'm not pestering you, am I?' and once again he laughed.

Then I asked him if he could sign the £5 poster for my daughter, Lucy (I knew he'd stopped signing stuff at this point, so I was being a bit cheeky). 'Oh John.' he said. 'Give us it here!' and he autographed it for her straightaway.

'I hear you've started to put all your old costumes on mannequins and that you're getting your old memorabilia together, for an exhibition,' I said, feeling it was time to finally come clean.

'Did you know I've still got your maraca?'

'Have you?' he said. 'Have you?' and he just looked at me dryly. 'John,' he said, 'Keep it.'

Angela then asked if she could take a photo of David, George and me, so he turned to a bloke behind him and said, 'I think you'll want one of these won't you?'

The bloke behind him turned out to be Mark Adams, who runs David's website and when he asked me for permission to put the photo on the website I obviously agreed.

While we were chatting a young man interrupted to talk to David. They seemed very close.

'I'll speak to you later,' he said to the young man, and then I cottoned on. It was, Duncan his son.

'Was that your lad?' I asked him. David nodded. 'How old is he now?'

'Thirty-one,' he replied.

'A year older than mine,' I said, by which time Duncan had left the room.

I didn't want to overstay my welcome, so I told David I'd better be on my way. He shouted to me as I was going through the door: 'John, keep in touch.' I answered, 'I will, I will.'

That was the last time I saw him alive.

Chapter 7
WHAT SURVIVES OF US

There were to be many tributes to Mick Ronson following his death in April 1993 and I was asked to play in several commemorative concerts both in London and Hull.

On 29 April 1994, I joined Benny Marshall, Tony Visconti, Ched Cheesman and John Bentley at the Hammersmith Odeon onstage to play a Rats reunion set. The tribute gig had been organised by Kevin Cann and Mick's sister Maggi, and we performed 'I Feel Free' and 'It Ain't Easy' (or as Mick might say, 'It's fucking easy!') to a packed audience. At the end the full cast of performers

Geoff Appleby on the stage with Ian Hunter at Hammersmith Apollo

came on stage for the encore, 'All the Young Dudes'. Ian Hunter led the vocals and everyone, including Bill Wyman, Roger Daltrey and Roger Taylor, were all out front for the final chorus.

As we were singing the final verse, I glanced across to the wings offstage and could see Geoff Appleby in the wings, now wheelchair-bound after a crippling brain haemorrhage. His wife Moira was standing close behind him. I thought, *Geoff should really be here with us,* so went over to get him. After all, he was both a former Rat and a member of The Hunter-Ronson band and had played on the hit single 'Once Bitten Twice Shy'. He deserved his place out front, and to be seen. He'd also been a close friend of Mick's and myself, and had been a part of both our musical histories over the years.

So I wheelbarrowed Geoff to centre stage, alongside Ian.

When Ian saw him, he said something like: '*Alroight* Geoff' and I felt glad I was able to do that for my old friend, on that special stage that had so much meaning and history.

As a postscript to this wonderful celebration of Mick Ronson's life, there was also a sad element. Mick Wayne, who I'd sent a last-minute ticket, evidently arrived just after our performance. Later I found and spoke to him in the auditorium and then went to get him a backstage pass. When I returned to get him I discovered he had left (he told me on the phone the next day that he reluctantly had to leave early). Sadly, this was the last contact I had with Mick.

A month or so later I received a call from Mick's daughter, Sarah, who told me the shocking news that Mick had just died in a house fire in America. I still think about him. I also think how poignant it was that my last face-to-face meeting with Mick Wayne was at Mick Ronson's memorial concert. Strange indeed.

On Saturday, 9 August 1997, another Mick Ronson tribute gig was held, this time at the Hull Ice Arena. One of the guest bands was Yellow Monkey, who are a huge rock band in Japan. They owe a great debt of influence to Ronno and Bowie (some of their records were also produced by Tony Visconti) and they have a massive following in their own country.

When Yellow Monkey played, there were possibly 600 Japanese fans in the audience. At the open-air, free gig in Queen's Gardens on the following day, there must have been even more. The city centre

Yellow Monkey in Queen's Gardens, 1997

bars had been virtually drunk dry by their enthusiastic and devoted Japanese followers.

During a break at the gig in Queen's Gardens (where Mick used to work as a gardener), I went with my friend Pete Alison to the Burlington Tavern for a pint. On our way back I couldn't help notice how excited and energetic these tourists were, considering how far they'd all travelled to see their idols live. As we were walking back across the grass towards the performance area, I stopped to talk to two of them, a boy and a girl, and said: 'Are you waiting for Yellow Monkey?', gesturing to the stage.

'Yes, yes,' they nodded, excitingly. So I waved my hands to say *Follow me*, which they did. The backstage area was only a temporary fence like the ones you see around building sites, with just one guy on security.

As we approached security with my 'artist' lanyard on, I said that the couple 'were with me' and he let them in. It just so happened that Yellow Monkey were sitting together on the wall opposite, so I looked at these two fans and pointed to them. They went absolutely daft with excitement, taking photographs, getting the band to sign autographs, and so on. I just went out and left them all to it

Pete Alison looked at me and said, 'Why did you do that?'

'Because I could,' I said.

In the audience at the final tribute gig at the Hull Ice Arena was an old mate of mine, Les Holdstock. Now, Les looks uncannily like David Bowie, and can also carry a fair tune. He had milked these combined assets over the years to become a well-known local Bowie tribute act (in fact, all the recent legendary sightings of Bowie in Hull were, in fact, Les!). I invited Les backstage to the VIP bar and as we walked in we clocked Ian Hunter and his band at a table not far from us. Ian glanced up and gave the most casual cool wave he could, acknowledging what he thought was the arrival of David – and for a while I think he was genuinely taken in!

For the 'All the Young Dudes' encore, I mischievously invited Les to join us on stage. He was wearing a striking white frilly shirt and really looked the part. The reaction of the Yellow Monkey fans when he stepped up was particularly unforgettable.

'Does he want a mic?' shouted the sound guys, also taken in.

It was a great way to end the show.

They say you should never meet your heroes, or you'll be disappointed. Many people, especially big Bowie fans, are in awe of

Les Holdstock with George Underwood

the fact that I lived and worked with him. Despite all the hype surrounding his career and the image that he projected through the media, to me he was always just a very decent, accessible and intelligent friend.

The glamorous world of the celebrity can seem so other-worldly unless you've experienced it yourself and in some way lived it. Having lived with David, there wasn't much that could ever faze me again, even though I did experience the odd moment of hero worship myself.

As you now know, I have many drummer heroes, but above all is the great American bandleader and jazz drummer Buddy Rich. Buddy played with many of the true greats of the twentieth century: Frank Sinatra, Ella Fitzgerald, Nat King Cole, Count Basie, Louise Armstrong and Artie Shaw. He was an incredible, highly influential jazz drummer. He was world famous for the Buddy Rich Big Band, with which he toured the world extensively with the Buddy Rich Big Band. Many of the world's top rock drummers – including John Bonham, Phil Collins, Roger Taylor and Carl Palmer – cite Buddy as an inspiration.

In the mid '80s, the Buddy Rich Big Band was appearing at Bridlington Spa Theatre, about twenty miles from where I live in Beverley. I'd played the Spa several times myself so I knew the layout, including dressing rooms and backstage area. I had taken my son Aaron who was only seven at the time as well as my friend Martin Rippingale, to keep an eye on Aaron (I hoped) while I tried to get Buddy's autograph for the collection. What a prize that would be!

We arrived about 5 p.m. and I asked at the front desk to see if Buddy was here yet. He wasn't, so we went round the back to the artist's entrance to wait. About an hour passed and there was still no sign of him, when the stage door suddenly opened and a very worried stage manager appeared, glancing up and down the road at the back of the theatre. I asked him if they were still going to appear that night and he said the band had been delayed and would probably be a bit late. Not long after, a large single decker bus pulled up at the stage door, and I could see Buddy there in the front seat behind the driver. He was one of the first to exit the bus, so I approached him with the autograph book which he happily signed to 'Cambo' and another one to my son Aaron.

Job done – or so I thought.

When we went round to the front of the theatre, we saw a man setting up a merchandise stall, selling albums. A signed Buddy Rich album would be an added bonus, so I bought two each with a good photo of him on the cover. I then went back round to the stage door where the crew and roadies were now frantically unloading all the gear in at high speed.

When I saw two Spa officials in uniform, I approached them and in my best American accent asked, 'Can you tell me which dressing room Buddy is in, please?'

Neither of them batted an eyelid and probably assumed I was with the band. They just pointed me to the corridor where the dressing rooms were. Now, completely immersed in the role, I asked if they could also tell me 'where the nearest café or burger bar was'.

'Thanks guys, and have a nice day,' I said, confidently heading to the dressing room area where Buddy's door was slightly open. I sort of crept in, only to see Buddy, looking completely knackered as a gentleman dresser combed his toupee (I never knew Buddy wore one!), so I just asked if he would just 'mind signing these' too. Once again, he willingly agreed – after all, these were albums and not just the back of a fag packet. On the way out, I even managed to add some of the band's signatures as well.

After a fantastic show, we hung around outside the stage door; I thought we'd be able to see the bus leave and wave them off. Everybody had boarded and the inside lights were on as people stacked the luggage racks and generally settled into their seats. I noticed Buddy was sitting in the same seat as when he arrived, just behind the driver with the front door wide open. As there was no way for the bus to turn around easily, meaning it would probably have to do a three- or even four-point turn, I had another brainwave. I'd get my programme signed too!

Like Spiderman, I confidently mounted the moving bus, only to be greeted by the thick sweet smell of dope. Everybody sat down hurriedly and faced the front, trying to look innocent and obviously thinking I was a plain clothes UK drugs officer about to do a raid.

So when I handed my programme to Buddy to sign, he looked up at me, slightly relieved, but also a bit quizzically as if to say, 'Don't I know you from somewhere?'

I jumped off the bus having secured my fifth Buddy Rich autograph of the night. This was my idol, but our meeting had grounded him a lot more, in my mind.

After all, I'd also seen him naked, so to speak – minus 'rug'.

I never thought of David as David Bowie 'the star'. That was not how I'd got to know him. There were no awkward moments or pauses in conversation, it was all very natural and relaxed.

Once I had mastered the technology and could confidently send and receive emails, David and I continued the correspondence between face-to-face meetings. Whenever we corresponded, it was never fan mail, as you can see from our banter below.

Here's a selection you might enjoy:

16 November 2009 8.50

Hi Dave,

I don't know if you have my email address or not, but this is my new one. How are you keeping? I had a guy come to see me last week with The Roundhouse gig film that we did in 1970. I didn't realise that Genesis were on first. He asked me did David use their Hammond organ to play Memory of A Free Festival? He was quite surprised when I told him it was small plastic organ bought from Woolies.

I also told him you were once busking in Oxford Street doing a mime routine with all the white greasepaint on, clown suit etc. When a policeman tried to move you on you carried on with the mime until he arrested you and said the immortal words 'You have the right to remain silent' (I made the last bit up, but it made me laugh!)

Well Dave I hope it's not another seven years before we see each other again. All the best to you and your family

John Cambridge

16 November 2009

Good to hear from you john ! Things ticking over slowly here but good. And you ?
db

11 January 2010 at 9.27 PM

Is this you john ?
Db

12 January 2010 at 16.29

Hi dave
Yes this is me (Cambo), Is that proof? Is everything ok with you, belated birthday greetings, all the best
John C

12 January 2010 at 11.53 AM

Hi dave
It's me again. I've just realised you must get a lot of emails from bogus people. If you ever want to give me a call for a chat anytime my number is
—. ****************** I'm sure you'll recognise my Hull accent.
JC

12 January 2010 at 4.56 PM

I'm still suspicious. How many moles do you have on the bottom of your left foot ?
How do you know this is me?
Who am I ? where am I?
What's happening ?
The 'real' db

12 January 2010 at 19.45

In answer to your questions.
Firstly: How did you know I had a bottom on my left foot?
Secondly : I'd know it's you because I'd recognise your typing anywhere
Thirdly: you are you and you are there and that's what's happening
This proves that I'm
JC

5 May 2012 at 15.22

Just dropping you a line to wish you a few happy christmas's and birthdays
How are you?, still driving ? I hope not!
But do you stay in hull for your summer hols as it's the seaside?
You wouldn't really have to go anywhere would you?
db

23 July 2014 at 3.37 PM

Hi Dave, just thought I'd drop you a keep in touch line. How are you keeping? fit and well I hope. I've just left a band called The Ceptionals. Now I'm an ex-Ceptional drummer

All the best, keep laughing

John Cambridge

23 July 2014 at 21.47

What the fuck are you doing with an ipad?
Give it back to that kid, pronto.
db

23 July 2014 at 5.27 PM
I will but stop calling me pronto.

John C

23 July 2014 at 22.30

That's a joke, surely
db

24 July 2014 at 4.05 PM
Ok, but Shirley is better than pronto
Jc

24 July 2014 at 13.04
On another note, how are you doing? Is your family/health good
And are you enjoying yourself?
I'm slowly writing and painting and lots of reading.
Great that you keep in touch John.
You know what I look like, how about a selfie of you looking like the old lag that you are?
david

24 July 2014 at 17.31
Hi Dave, here's the selfie, yes it's me and not my dad. We are all in good health thanks apart from the usual ailments. I have glasses for reading but no deaf-aid yet. I'm still playing in a local band and we're very big in Lilliput. I should have kept in touch more over the years but I didn't want you to think I was pestering you.
We'll keep in touch now, or if you get the urge to phone for a chat my number is ***************.
All the best
John

David must have known he had advanced liver cancer at the time he sent these last two emails. He had kept the news very private apart from a small circle of people close to him. It was kind of him to ask after my family when goodness knows what must have been going through his mind about his own health then.

I hear that he made a little pilgrimage to London just before his death. He went to visit a lot of our old haunts to show his daughter Lexi and wife Iman where he had grown up, lived and where we had played a lot of those early gigs.

He even took them on the London Eye.

The last time I heard from him, apart from his annual Christmas card on 7 December 2015, was less than a month before he died.

John 'Hutch' Hutchinson had recently published his book *Bowie & Hutch* and I managed to get a photograph of the two of us, his old 'Yorkie' mates, with Hutch holding a copy to the camera.

7 December 2015 at 11.21 AM

Do you recognise these old gits ?

7 December 2015 at 11.27
Re Yorkies
Stig backwards ! lol!!!

Db

My son Aaron rang me about 7 o'clock in the morning of 10 January, 2016.

'Dad, did you know David Bowie's died?'

With John 'Hutch' Hutchinson – the photo of the 'two old gits' John sent to
David just before his death in 2015

He was on his way to work and had just heard. I went to put
the telly on straight way, and it was on every channel. Then I had a
phone call from Radio Humberside to see if I could do an interview
over the phone.

I was going to the doctor for a blood test that morning so I
had to say no. Besides, I was glad that I had some time to collect
my thoughts. I wouldn't be back until 10.30, so they agreed to ring
me then. When they did, I spoke to David 'Burnsy' Burns, a local
radio presenter, but I was quite cut up and couldn't speak. I had a
lump in my throat. 'I'll give you a minute, John,' Burnsy said. 'I'm
really sorry'.

I just didn't know what to say.

Then *BBC Look North* contacted me for a piece on their TV
news show. Given the strength of the Hull–Bowie connection they
wanted a few words from me, but once again, I just didn't know
what to say.

It was all so unexpected. I can only assume I was in shock. I'd
had a Christmas card and email only a couple of weeks earlier.

And now he was gone.

There would be no more stories.

P.S.

Oh well, in the words of a great American storyteller,* 'That's all I have to say about that.' I really hope this book has achieved what I set out to do at the beginning – tell the story of a quite remarkable part of my life and at the same time clear up a few contradictions.

I've deliberately not included everything I've done in my life and career, as I'm sure a lot of it would bore the arse off most readers. I've just tried to stick to the main focus, and to see my friendship with David in particular as a story with a beginning, a middle and (for now) an end.

I hope our 2020 lockdown activity has not been a complete waste of time!

If you ever happen to see me out in Hull or Beverley at any Rebel gigs – my current band, Rejuvenated Elderly Blokes Enjoying Life – or at the *Turn and Face the Strange* stage show, don't be shy of coming over for a chat. Hopefully you will be bringing a copy of this book for me to sign too!

If by chance you see any early '60s *Beano* annuals, in some charity shop or at a carboot sale, maybe a bit scratched and scuffed, looking like a boy's former makeshift drum kit, or maybe even with 'Cambo' written on the inside, please put them aside for me! I'd love to add them to my memorabilia collection. And maybe in a few years this book might be there with them!

And finally, finally, if you ever decide to do what I've done and to write something like this yourself, maybe even your own life story, I hope you found my dad's wise words useful about how to make it more 'marmalade'. Just remember, never use a big 'lighthouse' because a diminutive 'wheelbarrow' will always suffice.

Cambo
2021

---

* Forrest Gump

Afterword
BREAKING – THE WIDTH OF A CIRCLE

David Bowie's 'latest' album *The Width of a Circle* was released on Parlophone Records on 28 May 2021, just as we were putting the final touches to this book. It is a really unique little collection of early Bowie recordings, photos and remixes taken mostly from the period when I was working with him and as we have described in this book.

In fact *The Width of a Circle* could almost be our companion soundtrack album!

The package is being marketed as the 2CD accompaniment to *The Metrobolist*, the album which was to eventually become known as *The Man Who Sold the World* and is packaged with an accompanying booklet with song-lyrics and letters, set-lists, remixes and previously unreleased tracks, including an early Mercury 'alternative mix' recording of that little song I listened to David compose, 'The Prettiest Star'. It also features *Sounds of the Seventies: the Andy Ferris Show* and music for a mime performance by David broadcast on Scottish TV in July 1970.

So here is Hype's complete recorded musical history, finally released in an official form, also including that complete Sunday Show introduced by John Peel recorded on 5 February 1970 which was later transmitted on 8 February and featuring the debut 'Hype' line-up of:

David Bowie – vocals, twelve string guitar and organ
Mick Ronson – guitar
John Cambridge – drums
Tony Visconti – bass

The 'Peel' set in its entirety consists of:

Amsterdam
God Knows I'm Good
Buzz the Fuzz
Karma Man
London Bye Ta Ta
An Occasional Dream
The Width of a Circle
Janine
Wild Eyed Boy from Freecloud
Unwashed and Somewhat Slightly Dazed
Fill Your Heart
The Prettiest Star
Cygnet Committee
Memory of A Free Festival

The first four acoustic songs were typically of a kind David would perform at his renowned Arts Lab nights at The Three Tuns in Beckenham, and were played on that Hagstrom 12-string guitar he so often left lying around Haddon Hall. I join David on drums after Karma Man and Mick, who, as you will know, had been barely with us a couple of days at this point, debuted on lead guitar from *The Width of a Circle* onwards.

I've really enjoyed the lovely comments made by others about my contribution to this phase, especially Tony's quote that '(I was) a fabulous drummer and a great human being. He had this Yorkshire ability to make you laugh.' It's nice of him to be so generous.

I think what is important is that we can see in this collection, the 'transition' period from the folk acoustic troubadour David was, to the rock front man he became. It is a significant turning point in the history of post-Beatles twentieth century music and though it may sound a bit raw and incomplete in places, for me it is evidence

of the direction David was heading, and I know that my small contribution was an important one.

A *Record Collector* magazine's article (May 2021) 'A Long, Long
Time Ago' explored this phase and the CD/book release and quoted
me saying 'The whole Hull connection was me. I wasn't a Spider,
but I did help weave the web.' I suppose it has been easier for other
people to see this better than I could myself.

It has also been great to see that, apart from the 'Memory of
a Free Festival' single and the *Space Oddity* album, these Hype's
recordings with me drumming are now released officially as a part
of the Bowie legacy.

Appendix I
JOHN CAMBRIDGE CAREER TIMELINE, 1964–2021

1964–66	The Gonx
1966	The Attack, The Hullabaloos (with Mick Wayne)
1966–67	ABC
1967–69	The Rats (changed to Treacle for a period, then back to The Rats)
1969–70	Junior's Eyes (including with David Bowie)
1970	Hype (with David Bowie)
1970–71	The Mandrakes
1971–72	The Locarno Ballroom (residency)
1972–73	The Harvey Brookes Band
1973–75	Hutch & It's Easy (Scarborough Penthouse) (The Geordie Scene – Tyne Tees)
1976	Various dep. gigs
1977	The Oven Pads (Mick Ronson's favourite name for a band!)
1977	Misty
1977–78	Dee Street Club (residency)
1978	Uncle Sam
1978–79	Tammy Cline and Uncle Sam
1979–80	Benny and the Jets (featuring Rats singer Benny Marshall)
1980–81	The Muff Divers

1981–83   Tammy Cline Band – touring (including with Max
          Boyce)
1983–   Various dep. gigs and residencies, including Small
          Change, Barry John and Dave Holley, Tammy Cline,
          Steve Powell, Phil Sinner, Scarlet Rainbow.
          Residencies at Trinity Club, Telstar Club, Ritz Club,
          The Swallow, The Forresters Arms, Distinction, The
          Springhead Pub, Southcoates Club, The Cellar Bar
          – Waterfront.
          The Commotions, The Remnants, Nightmoves,
          The Muff Divers, Black Pearls, Mean-Eyed Cat, Tin
          Soldier, Rebel.
2017–21   *Turn and Face the Strange – The Mick Ronson Story*,
          Hull Freedom Centre, Hull Truck Theatre, London
          Marble Arch, Central Synagogue.

A TYPICAL GONX SET

(Some of these were the artists' versions of songs, and not their own compositions.)

The Beatles
Money
Roll Over Beethoven (the Beatles' version, Chuck Berry wrote the song)

The Rolling Stones
You Can't Judge a Book by the Cover
Mona (I Need You Baby)
It's All Over Now
Not Fade Away
I'm a King Bee
You Better Move On

The Kinks
All Day and All of The Night
Beautiful Delilah
Long Tall Shorty
You Really Got Me
Louie Louie
I Gotta Move

Various

Love Potion No. 9	The Searchers
Talkin' About You	The Searchers
By the Way	The Big Three
Poison Ivy	The Coasters
Spoonful	The Rats
Pretty Thing	Bo Diddley
Memphis, Tennessee	Chuck Berry
Rosalyn	The Pretty Things
Untie Me	Manfred Mann

.

Appendix III
A TYPICAL RATS SET

(Once again these were the artists' version of the song.)

Jeff Beck (who else?)
Tallyman
Rock my Plimsoul
Jeff's Boogie
Hi Ho Silver Lining
Wee Wee Baby
Shapes of Things
Love is Blue
Morning Dew
Rock Me Baby
You Shook Me
Telephone Blues
I Ain't Superstitious

Jimi Hendrix
Burning of the Midnight Lamp
Spanish Castle Magic
Wait Until Tomorrow
You Got me Floatin'
Fire
Stone Free

Cream
Spoonful
Sunshine of Your Love
NSU

The Beatles
It Won't Be Long
Paperback Writer
Sgt. Peppers Lonely Hearts Club Band

Various, including:

Brothers Six	Some Kind of Wonderful
The Miracles	Going to a Go-Go
Don Covay	Mercy, Mercy
The Byrds	So You Want To Be a Rock 'n' Roll Star
Moby Grape	Hey Grandma
Gladys Knight & The Pips	Stop and Get a Hold of Myself

Appendix IV
HYPOLOGY TIMELINE

1970 Hype gigs (David Bowie, Mick Ronson, Tony Visconti, John Cambridge)

Tuesday 3 February	The Marquee Club London
Thursday 5 February	Paris Studios London (John Peel's show *Top Gear* – first gig with Mick Ronson)

David and Angie come to stay in Hull at my mum and dad's. Mick Ronson works his notice as a council gardener, Tony Visconti and Liz Hartley stay in Beverley. David rings around to get work!

Sunday 22 February	The Roundhouse, Chalk Farm, London
Saturday 28 February	The Arts Centre, Basildon
Sunday 1 March	The Arts Lab, The Three Tuns, Beckenham
Tuesday 3 March	The White Bear, Hounslow
Friday 6 March	Hull University
Saturday 7 March	London Polytechnic
Wednesday 11 March	The Roundhouse, Chalk Farm. London (the 'dressing up' gig, supported by some up and coming group called Genesis)
Friday 13 March	The Locarno Ballroom, Sunderland

Monday 30 March	The Star Hotel, Croydon (my last gig with Hype)

1969–70 Recording Sessions

Wednesday 16 July 1969	Trident Studios, London
Monday 8 September	Trident Studios, London (double session)
Tuesday 9 September	Trident Studios, London
Thursday 11 September	Pye Studios, London
Tuesday 16 September	Trident Studios, London
Monday 20 October	BBC Dave Lee Travis Radio Show, London
Friday 19 December	Marquee Studios, with Kevin Westlake
Thursday 5 February 1970	BBC John Peel Show, Paris Studios, London
Monday 23 March	Trident Studios, London
Wednesday 25 March	Andy Ferris/Dave Symonds Radio Show Playhouse Theatre, London

1970 Recording session with Marc Bolan
(Dib Cochran & The Earwigs)

24 March 1970	London Weekend TV Studios

Appendix V
CAMBOLOGY TIMELINE 1970

6 January David says: 'I like your drumming and I like you as a person' as I am offered the position of drummer in David's new band.

8 January I play the Speakeasy Club as David's drummer with Tony Visconti and David.

25 January After playing in Germany with Junior's Eyes, I return to Hull and try to recruit Mick Ronson for Hype. He reluctantly agrees to join me (once he'd finished marking out his football pitches). We travel back to London in my Hillman Minx on 3 February.

3 February Junior's Eyes plays their farewell gig followed by Hype's debut set at the Marquee Club, Soho. I play drums for both bands and Mick Ronson watches both gigs. Afterwards I introduce him to David and we go back to Haddon Hall, where Mick and David talk, rehearse and swap musical ideas.

4 February Mick and David continue rehearsing. Mick Ronson is asked by David to join the band for John Peel's imminent *Top Gear* show.

5 February Mick plays John Peel's *Top Gear* show with us, and from his comments live on radio, it's clear that David is very keen to have Mick join us more permanently.

A couple of days after the gig we travel back to Hull so David can have his car serviced in Hessle and Mick can sort out his affairs ready to join Hype at Haddon Hall. David and Angie stay in Hull, with my parents, and Tony and Liz stay with my fiancée Angela's parents in Beverley, along with Angela and myself.

22 February Hype play their first big gig at the Roundhouse, together with Mick Ronson.

23 February Angie writes to my Mam and Dad following their stay, saying 'I am blooming' and promising to 'see you soon'. Mick returns to Haddon Hall to live and begins to seriously work with David.

23 March Recording 'Memory of a Free Festival (Parts 1&2)' at Trident Studio. We were booked in from 11 pm. to 4 am.

We complete the recording, with Ronno adding backing vocals to the 'Yeah, yeah, yeah' chorus at the end. Marc Bolan popped into Trident while we were recording and was asked if he wanted to join in the chorus section of 'Memory of a Free Festival'. Strangely enough, Bowie did not sing in the choir section with Bolan, I did.

Ronno loses his temper with me in the studio for not being able to get the drumming for a new part he has written for David's new song 'The Supermen'. 'Come on, it's fucking easy!' he shouts.

24 March 1970 Tony Visconti books me to play on Marc Bolan's Dib Cochran & the Earwigs single 'Oh Baby' at London Weekend Television Studios.

25 March Ken Pitt later writes about turning up at the studio and realising that, from the 'look on Mick Ronson's face', he is about to be sacked.

3 April 1970 I find out many years later that Woody Woodmansey, Mick Ronson and Tony Visconti sign a predated contract for Hype with Philips Records.

6 April 1970 David tells me while I am 'climbing the ladder of success' (painting the ceiling in Haddon Hall) that they are replacing me in Hype. He lends me £5 to get back to Hull.

7 April 1970 I pack my things and leave Haddon Hall at 8.30 am. Despite the obvious loud sounds and banging about, no one stirs to give me a hand to load up. I stop on the way in Notting Hill to buy two premium bonds with the £5 David has lent me to get home.

Forty-two days after joining Hype, with what seemed like the world at my feet, I am unemployed and heading up the A1, back home to Hull.

Appendix VI
WHO'S WHO

Appleby, Geoff (ex-Rats, Hunter Ronson bass player)

Bolder, Trevor (bass player for the band Ronno and The Spiders from Mars)

Burns, Terry (Bowie's elder half-brother)

Cann, Kevin (Bowie authority, author and designer)

Cattini, Clem (famous sixties/seventies session drummer)

Chapman, Michael (Hull-based folk singer/guitarist who gave Mick Ronson his first recording break)

Cheesman, Keith 'Ched' (Rats' bass guitarist, lead guitarist in *Turn and Face the Strange*)

Cline, Tammy (country and western singer)

Cornell, Pat (owner of Cornell's Music Store, Hull, who sold Mick his famous Les Paul guitar)

Cousins, Dave (lead singer of The Strawbs)

Defries, Tony (David Bowie and Mick Ronson's manager, head of Mainman)

Dudgeon, Gus (renowned record producer, 'Space Oddity' single producer)

Elliot, Bobby (drummer The Hollies)

Farthingale, Hermione (member of the Bowie trio Feathers, along with John 'Hutch' Hutchinson)

Farr, Brian (Hull-based musician and friend)

Gardner, Dave (lead singer, The Gonx)

George, Stuart 'Stuey' (roadie and bouncer for The Rats, Bowie and many others)

Hartley, Liz (Tony Visconti's girlfriend, resident of Haddon Hall)

Herd, Keith (owner of Fairview Studios, Willerby near Hull, Producer of 'Bernie Gripplestone')

Hunter, Ian (lead singer Mott the Hoople, Hunter-Ronson)

Hutchinson 'Hutch', John (East Yorkshire-based guitarist singer, member of Bowie's band Feathers)

Irvine, Denise (Mick Ronson's former fiancé, mother of his first son Nicholas)

Jones Haywood Stenton, John (Bowie's father)

Jones, Margaret 'Peggy' (Bowie's mother)

Garson, Mike (pianist with David Bowie)

Kelly, Graham 'Grom' (lead singer with Junior's Eyes)

Kemp, Rick (bass player with Steelye Span, manager of Hammonds Music department, Hull)

Lee, Albert (renowned session guitarist)

Lodge, John 'Honk' (bass player with Junior's Eyes)

Lowe, Andy Fairweather (lead singer with Amen Corner, also had a hit with 'Wide Eyed and Legless')

Mace, Ralph (musician, played the Moog on 'Memory of a Free Festival'*)*

Manning, Bernard (comedian)

Marriot, Steve (lead singer with The Small Faces)

Marshall, Benny (lead singer with The Rats)

Mirkin, Pete (Hull friend and Rats' roadie, as well as being the mechanic who serviced Bowie's car)

Nicol, Les (Hull-based lead blues guitarist)

Palmer, Alan (later Robert Palmer, became world famous for singles like 'Addicted to Love')

Pitt, Ken (David Bowie's manager from 1967–70 prior to Ziggy Stardust)

Powell, Steve (Bass guitar, The Gonx)

Reeves, Gabrels (guitarist with David Bowie)

Renwick, Tim (session guitarist, guitarist with Junior's Eyes)

Rich, Buddy (world-famous drummer and band leader)

Riley, Marc (ex-band member of The Fall, BBC DJ/presenter)

Ronson, Maggi (Mick Ronson's sister)

Shenstone, Clare (actress and friend of David and Angie)

Simpson, Jim (original Rats drummer)

Taylor, Clive 'Spud' (former Rats' drummer)

Underwood, George (artist, friend of Bowie's who caused Bowie's pupil to dilate after a fight)

Wayne, Mick (lead guitarist with The Hullabaloos, Junior's Eyes, Bowie)

Woodmansey, Mick Woody 'Pecker' (drummer with The Roadrunners, The Rats, Bowie)

BIBLIOGRAPHY

Bowie, David and Rock, Mick, *Moonage Daydream: The Life and Times of Ziggy Stardust* (Cassell, 2005).

Cann, Kevin, *David Bowie: Any Day Now: The London Years, 1947–1974* (Adelita, 2010).

Gillman, Peter and Leni, *Alias David Bowie* (Henry Holt, 1987).

Gilly, Karen, and Weird, *Mick Ronson: The Spider with the Platinum Hair* (Independent Music Press, 2003).

Goddard, Simon, *Ziggyology: A Brief History of Ziggy Stardust* (Ebury Press, 2013).

Goodard, Simon, *Bowie Odyssey 70* (Omnibus Press, 2020).

Hiatt, Brian (ed.), *A Portrait of Bowie*: A Tribute to Bowie By His Artistic Collaborators and Contemporaries' (Hachette, 2016).

Hutchinson, John, *Bowie & Hutch* (Lodge Books, 2014).

Jones, Dylan, *David Bowie: A Life* (Windmill Books, 2017).

Morley, Paul, *The Age of Bowie* (Simon & Schuster, 2016).

Pitt, Ken, *David Bowie: The Pitt Report* (Design Music Ltd, 1983).

Sandford, Christopher, *David Bowie, Loving the Alien* (Warner Books, 1996).

Tremlett, George, *David Bowie – Living on the Brink* (Century, 1996).

Trynka, Paul, *Starman: David Bowie* (Sphere, 2011).

Visconti, Tony, *Bowie, Bolan and the Brooklyn Boy* (Harper Collins, 2007).

Woodmansey, Woody, *Spider from Mars: My Life with Bowie* (Pan Macmillan, 2016).

PHOTOS AND ILLUSTRATIONS

Dad and Mam Cambridge with son Aaron

John with brother Ken

John – Cowboyman Jnr

J.P. Cornells, Hull (1964), the shop where John bought his first Trixon drum kit and later his Ludwig drums. Mick Ronson also bought his famous Gibson Les Paul custom here

The Gonx – on the steps in Scarborough. Back row, L-R Steve Powell, Dave Carmichael, John Rowe. Front row, L-R Dave Gardner, John Cambridge

A Gonx newspaper article, c.1965

The Beatles – from when John went to see them at the A.B.C in Hull

ABC 1966, L-R John Rowe, Rick Hebblethwaite, John Cambridge, Les Nicol, Steve Powell

ABC 1967 (Mark 2) L-R John Cambridge, Les Nicol, Mike Tyson, Rick Hebblethwaite

Gig posters: The Gonx at Skyline 1965, The Gonx at Malton 1965, The Rats 1968, ABC 1965, Hullaballoos at Spa 1965 (signed by Mick Wayne)

John in full mid-60s posing gear in 1968 (Treacle). Clothes from Carnaby Street, from Don Lill, Treacle's manager

Treacle. The Rats, briefly, by another name

The Rats on holiday going swimming! Summer of 1968. L-R Mick Ronson, Eric McMinn, Chris Adamson, John Cambridge

The Rats at The Duke of Cumberland Pub in Ferriby 1968 – John Cambridge, Benny Marshall, Ched Cheesman, Mick Ronson

John with Stuart 'Stuey' George

The Rise and Fall of Bernie Gripplestone, handwritten lyrics

Dad Cambridge's directions to Scoulton, Norfolk to meet Junior's Eyes

Junior's Eyes, London, summer of 1969. L-R John 'Honk' Lodge, John Cambridge, Mick Wayne, Tim Renwick, Grom Kelly

David Bowie in late 1968, about the time that he wrote 'Space Oddity'

The Phoenix Club, Hessle Road. The only other venue David Bowie played in Hull. During his stay in 1970 David played bingo with John, Jim Simpson (and Jim's dad), one Sunday lunchtime – just before the stripper!

Angie Bowie's letter to Mam and Dad, February 1970

Star Hotel advert; John's last gig with Bowie

Bowie and Hype articles from John's scrap book, March 1970

The Haddon Hall stepladders on which John was sacked!

The Premium Bond John bought on the way home after being sacked on the 7 April 1970

Letter from Tony Visconti (asking for David's fiver back!)

Letter from Mick Ronson

John playing with The Mandrakes at The Lord Mayors Hall in Paris, 1971. First band since returning home

Tammy Cline & Uncle Sam. L-R Lynn Blakeston, Tammy Cline, John Cambridge, Rod Boulton, Tony Beasty

'Hutch and It's Easy' at Tyne Tees studio's Newcastle, 1975. Appearing on the TV Programme called *The Geordie Scene*

Bowie autograph at the Tin Machine gig, 1989

Hull Daily Mail article, 1989. Reunion with Bowie at the Tin Machine gig

Letter from Iman Bowie asking for John's contribution to her special book, a gift to David for his 50th birthday

Tony helping to create Ziggy Sawdust!

David's reply letter to John's daughter's wedding invite 47

Geoff Appleby on the stage with Ian Hunter at Hammersmith Apollo

Yellow Monkey in Queen's Gardens, 1997

Les Holdstock with George Underwood

With John 'Hutch' Hutchinson – the photo of the 'two old gits' John sent to David just before his death in 2015

Cartoon by Lucy Cambridge, 2021

Colour section

1. David and John in a pre-match pose in the garden of Haddon Hall (photobombed by Nita Bowes, now Nita Clarke)

2. David, John and Angie Bowie (with a few 'neighbours') in the garden of Haddon Hall, Southend Road, Beckenham

3. David photographed by his manager, Ken Pitt, in a park close to Pitt's central London apartment in Manchester Street

4. Mick Ronson arrives at Haddon Hall (John is having a haircut just left of shot)

5. David, Mick and John strumming guitars at Haddon Hall

6. David playing some of his songs to Mick and John at Haddon Hall

7. Bowie and The Hype gig at The White Bear pub in Hounslow

8. Bowie, Tony Visconti and John at The Hype's famous early glam rock performance at The Roundhouse. Taken by Ray Stevenson, March 1970

9. Two more Ray Stevenson Roundhouse photos, the bottom including Mick as 'Gangster Man', March 1970

10. Backstage at the Tin Machine gig in Bradford in 1989. David looking like he's getting ready to play cricket for Yorkshire!

11a. Ched Cheesman, Tony Visconti, John Cambridge, Benny Marshall and John Bentley rehearsing for the Mick Ronson memorial gig at Hammersmith in 1994

11b. Reunion between Mick Wayne and John

12. The invitation to David's 50th birthday party in New York, complete with striking self-portrait illustration, January 1997

13a and 13b. David and John reunite at the 50th birthday party

14a. George Underwood and John at the 50th birthday party, David does some photobombing!

15a. Joe Elliott and John at the after-show party following the Hull Ice Arena gig, 1997

15b. Filming a sequence with Gary Kemp for the Sky Arts, Mick Ronson *Passions* documentary in 2016

16a. Once again with David and George Underwood, this time backstage at Hammersmith, 2002

16b. John, circa 2019, fending off blood-thirsty fans

Cartoon by Lucy Cambridge, 2021

ACKNOWLEDGEMENTS

The following are good friends I have played with, worked with and socialised with, in some cases for 50 years:

Ray Acaster, Geoff Appleby, Tony Beasty, Lynn Blakeston, Ian Bolder, Rod and Marilyn Boulton (Tammy Cline), Bri' Buttle, Kevin Cann, Alan Carey, Keith 'Ched' Cheesman, Ian 'Taffy' Evans, Brian Farr, Brian Gadie, Stuey George, Ian 'Gibbo' Gibson, Pete Green, John Hawley, Mick Kerry, Eric Lee, Brian Levitt, Denny Mac, Nick Oxlade, Steve Powell, Gus Ridley, Brian Rudd, Jim Simpson, Pete Smith, Steve 'Mally' Smith, Paul Sutton, Clive 'Spud' Taylor, Steve Trice, Danny and Duncan Wood, Andy Woonton and Steve Wright.

And to those who have sadly passed away:

Mam and Dad, my brother-in-law David Nixon, Pete Alison, Steve Seaton, Dave Nicholson, Mick Wayne, John 'Hutch' Hutchinson and, of course, David Bowie.

A big thanks to my daughter Lucy for the original cover idea and for all her great work in organising and enhancing the images.

A special thank you to my friend Garry Burnett, who has been pestering me for three years to do this book. Without his great help, it would never have happened.

And finally, I would like to thank Kevin Cann for his advice, keen eye on the detail and expertise in all things Bowie.